THE
SERPENT
SLAYER

AND OTHER STORIES OF
STRONG WOMEN

THE
SERPENT
SLAYER

AND OTHER STORIES OF
STRONG WOMEN

Retold by KATRIN TCHANA

Illustrated by
TRINA SCHART HYMAN

 Little, Brown and Company
Boston   New York   London

For Sally, Sally, and Holle

K.T.

For Katrin, changing girl

T.S.H.

First Edition

Library of Congress Cataloging-in-Publication Data

Tchana, Katrin.
The serpent slayer ; and other stories of strong women/ retold by Katrin
Tchana ; illustrated by Trina Schart Hyman. — 1st ed.
p.   cm.
Summary: A collection of eighteen traditional tales from various parts of
the world, each of whose main character is a strong and resourceful
woman.
ISBN 0-316-38701-0
1. Tales.   2. Women — Folklore.   [1. Folklore.   2. Fairy tales.
3. Women — Folklore.] I. Hyman, Trina Schart, ill.   II. Title.
PZ8.1.T19Se   2000
[398.2] — dc20   95-35077

10   9   8   7   6   5   4   3   2   1

TWP

The paintings for this book were done in ink and acrylic on Strathmore paper. The text was set in
Meridien, and the display type is Galahad Regular with a Pabst initial cap.

Printed in Singapore

CONTENTS

Preface

ix

The Serpent Slayer

1

The Barber's Wife

7

Nesoowa and the Chenoo

13

Clever Marcela

19

Sister Lace

25

The Rebel Princess

31

Beebyeebyee and the Water God

37

Kate Crackernuts

43

The Old Woman and the Devil

47

The Magic Lake

53

Grandmother's Skull

61

Three Whiskers from a Lion's Chin

67

Duffy the Lady

71

Sun-Girl and Dragon-Prince

77

Staver and Vassilissa

85

Tokoyo

91

The Lord's Daughter and the Blacksmith's Son

97

The Marriage of Two Masters

105

Source Notes

111

Acknowledgments

113

PREFACE

Where do fairy tales come from? Fairy tales are stories told by everyday people, stories that parents tell their children, that the village elders tell before the fire at night. Originally they were oral stories, passed on by word of mouth, but now that so many people in the world know how to read and so many books are being printed, many of them have been written down. All of the stories in this collection were found in books and then re-told. They were changed a little, just as an oral storyteller will change a story that she first heard from someone else to make it more vivid and vital to her audience.

This book is a collection of fairy tales that are — sort of — from around the world. *Sort of,* because there aren't stories here from every country in the world or even every continent. But when we were looking for stories, we did try to find ones that traditionally came from many different places. Interestingly, the same story may often be found in many different cultures. For example, the story that in this collection is called "Clever Marcela" has been told in Europe, Asia, Africa, South America, and in the Pacific Islands. The heroine isn't always called Marcela, of course. In China her name is Plum Jade, and in the Czech Republic her name is Manka, but the story of a clever girl who outwits the king (or chief or magistrate or burgomaster) is an old, old tale found in many lands.

The stories in this collection are about women and girls who find themselves in difficult circumstances and respond in brave, clever, and thoughtful ways. Most collections of folk and fairy tales are collections of stories that remind us how to be heroes. But these stories are all about heroines. A heroine's experience is different from that of a hero's, for woman's experience of life through the ages has been different from man's. We believe we need more books that reflect that experience. These are stories that remind us how to be strong, adventuresome, creative women. They teach us how to survive enormous suffering and come out alive with our eyes shining and our feet kicking.

This book was put together by a daughter for her mother and by a mother for her daughter. It is meant to be a collection that will be read by mothers to their daughters, daughters to their mothers, and sisters to each other. It is also a book for women to read to the men who love them and to the boys they love, so that people everywhere remember the courage, strength, ingenuity, and intelligence that is every woman's heritage.

THE SERPENT SLAYER

 n the dark time of the year, when the days are short and a cold wind blows from the north, a serpent came to live in an old cave on the mountain of Yung Ling. This serpent was longer than the longest street in the village at the mountain's foot and wider than an ox and cart. Wherever it slithered, it left behind a trail of poisonous slime that turned the earth black and lifeless.

The serpent fed on any flesh it could find — fish, birds, deer, rabbits, and the occasional villager who happened to stray too close to its lair. Soon it had devoured all the animals on the mountain and began to make forays into the farms and fields of the villagers, stealing away their livestock. The people were terrified and called on the magistrate to act quickly, before their entire town was destroyed.

The magistrate, who was just as frightened of the serpent as the rest of the villagers were, had no idea what to do. In desperation he called for a sorcerer. That is how the sorcerer called Qifu the Greedy came to Yung Ling, eager to profit from the people's misfortune.

Qifu arranged for the magistrate to pay him an exorbitant fee, and he demanded that the villagers lodge him in the largest house in Yung Ling and supply him daily with the finest wines and all manner of delicacies to eat. After being assured that he would be well provided for, he locked himself in the house, explaining that he would need three days and three nights to meditate on the villagers' problem.

When the three days had passed, Qifu emerged from his house looking very solemn. "The serpent has come to Yung Ling as a punishment for the secret evil thoughts of the villagers. It demands sacrifice," he announced. "For three days and three nights I have spoken with the serpent in my dreams. I have felt the fire of its breath, smelled its terrible stench. On your behalf, I made a bargain with the mighty worm. Each year, on the first day of the eighth month, you must send it a maiden from the village. In exchange for the maiden, the serpent agrees to leave you in peace. Otherwise, it will destroy you all."

The villagers were horrified at the idea of sending their daughters to feed the serpent. But they were in awe of the powerful sorcerer, and no one dared to question him, especially after the magistrate publicly congratulated Qifu for his wise plan. And so every year on the first day of the eighth month, a fourteen-year-old girl was chosen by lottery and forced to climb the barren mountain to offer herself to the serpent. The girls were eaten alive by the voracious snake, and their families were so frightened that they didn't even dare climb the mountain to retrieve their daughters' bones and give them a proper burial.

Now, this arrangement pleased Qifu very much, for he had put himself in charge of the lottery. The villagers reimbursed him handsomely for his work and allowed him to continue living in his grand house. Furthermore, he soon grew rich on bribes taken from wealthy families who didn't want their daughters sent off to the mountain to be eaten alive by the terrible serpent. Then he would seek out one of the families so poor that they had no money to feed all their children anyway, and he would persuade them to give up one of their daughters in exchange for a small fee.

For the people of Yung Ling, it was as if a black cloud had permanently settled over their village. Yet the serpent bothered them very little now, only occasionally coming down the mountain to steal an ox or pig for itself, and no one knew what else to do, so they accepted this sad condition as their fate.

The sacrifices continued for nine years, until the year that Li Chi turned fourteen. Li Chi was the daughter of a poor family, and she had grown up watching her neighbors and cousins be sent off, year after year, to feed the hungry serpent. The longer she thought about how these young, innocent girls were required to sacrifice their lives before they had even begun to live, the angrier she became. At last she decided that it was time somebody did something about this snake, and since no one else seemed willing to do it, she realized she must take action herself.

As the day of the lottery drew near, Li Chi went to her parents and bowed respectfully. "Dearest Father and Mother," she said, "I have decided to offer myself to the serpent this year. Then the sorcerer will give you money. Also, there will be one less child to feed, and you won't have to pay my dowry."

Her parents were horrified, of course, and forbade her to speak of it again. But Li Chi was determined, and she secretly went to Qifu and told him that she wished to be chosen for the sacrifice. Qifu was delighted: With every passing year, it became more and more difficult to find girls from poor families, and cajoling the parents into giving up their daughters was always so unpleasant. He quickly sent a small sum of money to Li Chi's parents to seal the bargain.

He even agreed to her odd request that the town officials give her a good sword, a fearless hunting dog, a parcel of food, a clay bowl, and some fire-making flint. So this foolish child thinks she can fight the serpent, he said to himself, laughing. What harm can it do? The serpent would devour her even if she went with an army of the emperor's strongest soldiers. If she imagines herself to be the people's savior, at least she will walk up the mountain without crying or screaming.

On the first day of the eighth month, Qifu led Li Chi slowly up the mountain path toward the serpent's cave. Qifu had grown so fat from rich living that it was difficult for him to walk, and when they were only halfway up the mountain, he pointed her in the right direction and turned back to the village. Li Chi continued alone, accompanied only by the little dog the magistrate had given her.

She knew she was approaching the serpent's den by the stench that hung in the air. The ground near the cave was black and sticky, and the air was hot from the giant worm's fiery breath. The dog growled in fear and pressed himself against Li Chi's leg. But Li Chi patted his head and murmured words of encouragement, and the brave little animal did not run away. Soon they rounded a turn in the path and saw before them the serpent's cave, a black malodorous pit in the side of the mountain. Inside, the serpent lay sleeping. The entire mountain seemed to shudder with the rhythm of its snoring.

Li Chi's heart was pounding, and she was afraid she would faint from the terrible smell. Gathering her courage, she took out her clay bowl, placed it on a flat rock near the entrance to the cave, collected some branches, and built a fire around it. Then she took from her parcel of food a jar of sweet flour, a pot of honey, and a lotus-wrapped packet of rice balls.

As her little dog watched with bright, curious eyes, Li Chi sprinkled the flour into the bowl. She poured the honey over it and mixed it with a stick. Then she added the rice balls to the syrup. Soon the air seemed to brighten with the delicious odor of cooking rice and honey.

The serpent, roused from his midday dreaming by the sweet scent, slithered to the cave's entrance. First his great head emerged, with eyes shining like palace mirrors, and then his enormous body hunched itself out of the cave.

Li Chi and her dog leapt to one side as the serpent launched itself in a great curling wave, then dove directly into the boiling stew.

With a horrible worm-scream, the serpent recoiled, twisting its ghastly head in pain and rage. At that moment the fearless dog sprang and bit off one of its eyes, scratching the other with his claws. The serpent screamed again and humped itself to attack, but before it could strike, Li Chi lifted her sword and brought it down with all her strength on the

serpent's head. Again and again she struck, until finally the head was severed from the serpent's body and rolled onto the bloody sand. With a great shudder, the enormous snake went limp.

Li Chi sank to the ground. Her face and body were covered with the disgusting blood of the serpent, and she was trembling with exhaustion and fear. Now that the snake was dead, she couldn't imagine how she had found the courage to kill it. For many hours she lay motionless on the side of the mountain, with her faithful dog beside her.

Finally, as the sun dipped behind the mountain, Li Chi gathered what little strength remained to her and forced herself to go into the serpent's den. There she gathered the bones of the nine girls who had come before her and died such terrible deaths. She tied them into her bundle and carried them back down the mountain so that their families could give them a proper burial.

But even when she showed the bones to the villagers, they did not believe her story. Only after Li Chi had led a few of the bravest men up the mountain path so that they could see the serpent's body with their own eyes did the villagers accept that it was really dead. Then there was great rejoicing in Yung Ling, and a celebration was held to honor the brave young girl who had freed them from the serpent's evil hold. Everyone attended except for Qifu the sorcerer, who had mysteriously disappeared after word of Li Chi's victory reached the village, and the magistrate, who lost his position and fell into disgrace.

The townspeople allowed Li Chi to keep her dog, of course, and from that day forward, he never left his mistress's side. Li Chi herself eventually married, had many children and more than fifty grandchildren, and lived to be a hundred years old. The people of Yung Ling have never forgotten her. To this day any visitor to Yung Ling is sure to hear the story of Li Chi the Serpent Slayer.

THE BARBER'S WIFE

n a small village in a land not too near and not too far away, there lived a barber who was exceedingly handsome. But as lazy and silly a man as this barber would be hard to find. Every day he went off to work in the village square, but instead of cutting hair and shaving beards, as a barber should, he spent his time gambling and telling stories with his friends. Every day he returned home to his wife with empty hands and empty pockets, until finally he found himself with nothing left in his house but his wife and his razor, both of whom were as sharp as sharp could be.

The barber's wife was a sensible woman named Amarjit. She loved her husband very much, for he was handsome and charming and knew how to make her laugh. But she was tired of pinching pennies and worrying about where their next meal would come from.

"So here you are again," she said to her husband, "without so much as a cup of rice to show for all the time you've spent in the village square. What are we to eat tonight? You know very well there's nothing in the house."

"Sweetheart, what can I say? Business is slow," her husband replied with a smile.

"It's plain as the pretty nose on your face that business will always be slow with you," snapped Amarjit. "Very well. If you can't earn a living at an honest trade, you'll have to beg. The maharajah is having a wedding feast this week. Go to the palace and ask him for something. It would be bad luck for him to refuse you."

The barber was not at all pleased with this idea, but Amarjit made it clear that she had no intention of starving to death. If he didn't at least try to bring something home for them, he knew she would leave him, and that was that. So he grumbled and complained but in the end went off to the palace to beg from the maharajah.

After waiting in line with the other beggars for many hours, the barber at last came before the maharajah and humbly asked him to give him something.

"Something?" inquired the ruler, raising an eyebrow. "What sort of thing are you looking for, my good man? Speak up!"

The silly barber had no idea what he should ask for. Stuttering and stammering, he could only repeat that he wanted something.

"Give him a plot of wasteland near his village," the maharajah ordered at last. The barber realized there was probably nothing he could do with a piece of wasteland, but his wife had told him to ask for something, and something he had received. Now at least, he said to himself, maybe she will let me have some peace.

"You idiot!" cried Amarjit when she heard the news. "Whatever are we going to do with a piece of wasteland? How can we plow it without any oxen? Why didn't you ask the prince for some money to buy bread? Are you crazy?"

Amarjit carried on like this, throwing dishes and screaming and shouting, until finally, realizing there was nothing to be done and she had better make the best of a bad bargain, she calmed herself and sat down to think of a plan.

Bright and early the next day, she set off to look at their piece of land. "Follow me," she told her husband. "Whatever I do, you do it, too. And whatever happens, don't speak to anyone who passes by. I'll do the talking today." She began walking all over the field, peering anxiously at the ground. Whenever anyone walked by, she would stare even more intently. Then she would suddenly pretend to be startled by the newcomer, and she would sit down and act as if she were doing nothing at all. Her husband did exactly the same.

Now, a band of thieves happened to pass by on that day. Thinking that this couple was behaving very strangely, they hid behind some trees to watch them. They soon decided there must be something special about the field, and one of the thieves went over to ask about it.

"Whatever are you doing?" the thief asked Amarjit.

"Oh, nothing, nothing at all," the clever woman answered, but the thief persisted until she reluctantly agreed to tell him her "secret."

"Promise you won't tell anybody," she pleaded, and the thief swore he was the most trustworthy man that ever walked this earth.

"Well," she began, "my grandfather left us this piece of land, and before he died, he buried a pot of gold here. But we don't know where he buried it, so we've been trying to find the exact place before we start digging. But please don't tell anyone. Someone might try to steal the gold."

"My lips are sealed," the thief assured her, and hurried away to tell his companions everything he'd heard. As soon as Amarjit and her husband had gone home, the band of thieves began digging in the field, looking for the pot of gold. All night long they dug and dug, until every inch of earth had been turned over three times. But when the sun came up, they still hadn't found the tiniest nugget of gold, and they went away tired and angry.

When the barber and his wife came back to their field that morning, it looked as though it had been plowed three times. Amarjit was delighted and went straight to the village to borrow some wheat to plant, promising the grain seller she would pay it back with interest. She planted the wheat in the beautifully tilled soil and tended it carefully. When harvesttime came, her crop was so successful that she paid back her debt, kept enough to feed herself and her husband, and sold the rest for a big bag of gold coins, which she hid in her mattress.

The thieves saw what had happened, and they were furious. They went to the barber's house and banged on the door. "We dug up that whole field for you," the leader of the thieves called to Amarjit. "Now pay us for our work."

"I told you there was a pot of gold in the ground, but you couldn't find it. Well, *I* did, and I'm not giving it away to you," said Amarjit, slamming the door in their faces.

"Look out for yourself, woman!" the thieves warned. "If you won't give us our share, we'll come and take it!"

That night one of the thieves crept into the house and hid himself in the closet, intending to wait until the barber and his wife went to sleep and then sneak off with all the gold pieces. But Amarjit noticed him lurking there and decided to trick him at his own game.

While she and her husband were eating dinner, she sighed loudly and said, "Those thieves came by today. I hope they don't find the bag of gold I hid under the curry in the pot standing by our door."

"What are you talking about?" her husband cried. "I thought you hid the gold in your —" But Amarjit kicked him under the table and put her finger to her lips. Then husband and wife went off to bed.

As soon as the house was quiet, the thief tiptoed out of the closet, grabbed the pot of curry standing by the doorway, and lugged it back to his friends waiting in the bushes nearby.

"Here it is, here it is," the thief whispered to his companions. "She said she hid the gold under the curry."

"Curry!" the other thieves murmured happily. "Let's eat before we divide up the gold. It was hungry work, waiting for you all this time."

The thieves couldn't see anything because it was very dark. Without looking, they all reached into the pot and greedily stuffed the curry into their mouths. But instead of putting chicken in the curry, Amarjit had made it with worms and slugs and spider's eggs and all the most disgusting things you can imagine. The robbers became horribly sick, with terrible stomachaches and fevers.

After this, the barber and his wife had some peace, for the thieves were all sick in bed for many weeks. Amarjit tended her field, and the barber went back to gambling in the village square. He even cut some hair and shaved a few beards every now and then, just to keep his clever wife happy.

The dry season came to the village, and it was too hot to sleep indoors. One night Amarjit and her husband dragged their mattresses outside and slept in the yard, where it was cool. They didn't worry about the thieves, for they thought they were still sick from Amarjit's curry.

But the thieves had all recovered. In fact, they were planning revenge on Amarjit for having tricked them twice and making them so ill on top of it. Seeing the barber's wife sleeping peacefully, they decided to seize their opportunity, so they picked up her bed and carried it away.

Amarjit woke to find herself carried along on the heads of four of the robbers. She trembled with fear, imagining what they might do to her, but she couldn't think of any way to escape. She was frantically wondering what to do next when the thieves paused for a moment under a banyan tree. Without thinking twice, Amarjit grabbed the branch hanging over her head and pulled herself into the tree, leaving the covers on the bed as if she were still lying on it.

"This bed is too heavy," one of the thieves who was carrying the mattress complained to his companions. "Why don't you others take a turn?"

The robbers began arguing among themselves about who would carry the bed. Finally they decided they'd carried it far enough for one night, and they lay down to take a rest under the banyan tree. The captain of the robbers stayed awake to keep watch on the barber's wife, whom he still believed was sleeping in the bed.

Suddenly Amarjit had an idea. Drawing her veil across her face, she began to sing very softly. The captain of the thieves looked up and was quite startled to see a woman sitting in the tree. In the light of the full moon, Amarjit looked just like a fairy. The captain was a vain man, who believed himself to be irresistibly handsome. He decided this fairy must have fallen in love with him. He puffed out his chest and strutted back and forth under the tree, waiting for the fairy to come down and declare her love. When she went on singing and took no notice of him, he stopped and called up to her, "Come down, my beauty. I won't hurt you."

"Ahh!" sighed Amarjit. She turned her head and sighed again, mournfully.

"What's the matter, my lovely?" the captain called softly, so as not to wake the other thieves. "You are a fairy. You have fallen in love with me — there's nothing wrong with that. I love you, too, you know."

"Oh, no," the fairy said with another sigh. "You don't really love me. You're just saying that."

"But I do!" the captain insisted. "How can I prove it to you?"

"Well," said Amarjit coyly, "if you really loved me, you would climb up into this tree and give me a kiss."

So the captain began to climb the slippery banyan tree. But as soon as he had reached the lowest branches, Amarjit began to shriek and rock back and forth, so that the tree shook wildly. The branch the captain was holding broke off, and he fell to the ground with a crash. Amarjit couldn't help it — she burst out laughing.

The band of thieves woke up with a start, to find their leader lying half-unconscious on the ground and a strange figure in white leaning over them from the tree, making strange, eerie noises.

"What happened? What happened?" they asked their leader, shaking him back and forth — which only made him feel worse. All he could do was groan and point to the tree.

"*Whooo, whoooo,*" howled Amarjit, flapping her veil.

Convinced that an evil spirit had come to punish them for all their misdeeds, the terrified thieves picked up their captain and began running as fast as their legs would carry them. They ran and ran until they reached the next village, and they never came back again.

Amarjit climbed down from the tree, put her mattress on her head, and walked quietly home with it. She used the gold to buy some oxen to plow her fields. Her crops always thrived, and she and her husband never went hungry again.

Nesoowa and the Chenoo

In the Old Time, when the world was young, Nesoowa and Toma left their people and went to hunt in a wild and lonely part of the North Woods. The North Woods was a dangerous place because of the Chenoos, terrifying evil creatures that roamed the forests in those days. Chenoos began as humans, but the evil in their hearts drove them mad, until they became cannibals who liked nothing better than to eat human hearts.

There were many Chenoos in the North Woods, so most people were afraid to go there. But Toma and Nesoowa were young and brave. They knew the hunting was good in the north and didn't believe anything could harm them.

One day, however, when Nesoowa was alone in the camp, she heard a rustling in the bushes as if some wild beast were thrusting its way through. Suddenly there appeared in the clearing a horrible creature. It was shaped like a man but was not a man; it was covered in leaves and pine needles, with cold, staring eyes. It was a Chenoo.

Nesoowa trembled with fear. The Chenoo had seen her, and now there was no way to escape. She had no weapons in the camp, and even if she had, she would never have been able to kill a Chenoo. Thinking quickly, she decided to try to trick him instead.

Stepping boldly into the clearing, Nesoowa held out her arms to the cannibal. "My father!" she cried joyfully. "Whatever happened to you? Why have you been gone so long?"

The Chenoo looked dumbstruck. He had expected tears and screaming and prayers. No one had ever spoken to him in such a loving tone of voice. He looked down at the woman in confusion.

"Dear Father," Nesoowa continued softly, "how tired and ill you look. Wash yourself in the brook, and I will bring you some of your son-in-law's clothes to wear."

This Chenoo, whose name was Elaak, actually was very tired and very ill. He had spent many days battling the strongest of all the Chenoos, the monster Winsit, until finally he had fled from the battle in defeat. Now his senses were dulled by exhaustion and the pain of his wounds. Too tired to protest, he went to wash himself in the stream. He put on the clothes Nesoowa gave him and settled himself by her fire.

Nesoowa offered him food, but he shook his head with a snarl. Not knowing what else to do, the young woman sat calmly by the fire and took out her beadwork, trying to behave as though everything were normal. Yet all the time she was thinking of Toma, who would be back any minute. If she could only find some way to warn him, then both of them could escape.

After a while, Nesoowa smiled gently at the Chenoo. "Dear Father," she said, "I'm going to get some wood for the fire." But when she rose to go outside, Elaak followed her. Taking the ax from her hand, he began chopping down all the trees that surrounded their camp. He swung the ax ferociously, and one tall pine tree after another fell in his path.

Nesoowa began to be afraid he would chop down all the trees in the forest. "Father!" she cried. "Stop now! That is enough!"

The Chenoo put down the ax and returned to his place by the fire. Now he had shown her that even though he was sick, he was still stronger than any man.

Soon Nesoowa heard Toma whistling through the trees. He was home from hunting. "Father," she said loudly, "it's your son-in-law. How happy he will be to see you."

When Toma appeared in the clearing, she ran to him, smiling. "Look, Husband," she said. "Father has returned. Come and welcome him."

Toma saw the Chenoo sitting by the fire and his heart filled with dread. He realized the great danger to both of them and quickly understood what his wife was trying to tell him. Continuing her deception, he greeted the Chenoo warmly. "We have been so worried about you, Father. Come and smoke a pipe with me. I have much to tell you."

Toma sat by the Chenoo for many hours, telling him the news of the hunt and all that had happened to them since they'd come to the North Woods. Elaak refused to eat or smoke a pipe, but finally, as he listened to Toma's calm, soft voice, he fell asleep. The couple huddled together and watched the Chenoo, afraid to move. In a whisper, Nesoowa told her husband how the cannibal had appeared that afternoon and what she had done. All night long they sat by the fire, too terrified to sleep or try to escape.

In the morning Elaak opened his eyes and fixed them with a cold stare. "Bring me tallow!" he roared. Nesoowa hurriedly heated a pot of tallow over the fire. When the tallow had come to a boil, the Chenoo snatched it from the fire and drank it down in one gulp.

Elaak sat back down by the fire and stared bitterly out into the forest. After a while he spoke. "I will stay here," he said. "Winsit will never think to look for me in the camp of a human being. In the spring I will be strong again. I will kill him and eat his heart. Then I will be the strongest of all the Chenoos."

All winter long Elaak stayed in their camp. He was sullen and morose. Every day Nesoowa cooked for them. She tried to act naturally, but she was tense and uneasy. Toma was afraid to leave her by herself with the cannibal, so he stopped going hunting. By midwinter, their supply of meat was finished.

Early one morning Elaak shook Toma awake with a growl. "Come," he muttered. "We'll go hunting together."

"Wait, my father," Nesoowa said, "I will give you something to help you." She made him a pair of snowshoes from ash wood and rawhide.

When Elaak put on the snowshoes, he could move through the snow as fast as the wind. Even Toma, who was young and strong, could hardly keep up with him. Elaak led him deeper and deeper into the forest.

They came at last to a place where a stream of quickly moving water bubbled up through the ice and snow. Elaak took off his snowshoes and began to do a strange dance on the snow. Soon the water started to heave and boil. A monstrous lizard crawled out of the stream, and Elaak cut off its head with one blow.

Toma had never seen such a creature before, and he was disgusted at the thought of even touching it. But the Chenoo built a fire and roasted some of the meat. Toma was afraid to offend him by refusing to eat, and when he tasted the lizard meat, he was surprised to find it delicious.

After they had eaten, Elaak threw the head and tail of the creature back into the stream. "They will grow into another lizard," he said. "The rest of the meat is for my daughter."

He tied his snowshoes back on his feet and put the body of the lizard on his head. "Come," he said, gesturing to Toma. "Let us go home to my daughter."

Toma tried to follow him, but the Chenoo was going so quickly, it was impossible for him to keep up. At last Elaak turned to him. "Can't you go any faster?" he asked.

"No!" Toma gasped.

"Then get on my shoulders."

Elaak carried Toma and the meat all the rest of the way back to Nesoowa. They were home long before dark.

At last spring came to the forest. The snow began to melt, and many birds returned from the south. One day Kakakooch the crow came with a message for Elaak.

"Winsit knows where I am," Elaak told Toma and Nesoowa. "He is on his way here now, coming to fight me. We will do battle, and one of us will die. When he comes, my

children, you must hide in the cave behind our lodge and stop up your ears with moss. The battle cry of the Chenoos is too terrible for human ears."

Then Elaak told Nesoowa to bring him the bundle he had brought with him on the first day he came to their lodge. He untied the bundle and held up a pair of dragon horns, golden bright, one with two branches and the other straight and smooth. He gave the straight one to Toma.

"There's magic in this horn," he explained. "If you plunge it into the ear of a Chenoo, it will kill him instantly. If I die in battle, you must use it to kill Winsit. Otherwise he will eat you both."

Elaak grasped the other horn in his hand, and magically he began to grow, until he became as tall as the highest pine tree. A tremendous rage came over him, and he began to howl for Winsit, picking up huge boulders and smashing them to the ground in anger, pulling tall trees out of the ground by their roots.

Toma held his wife close. "Wife," he whispered, "now we have a weapon that can destroy a Chenoo. If Elaak is the loser, we will use it against Winsit. But if Winsit dies, we must kill Elaak."

Nesoowa caught her breath. She had shared her home with Elaak all winter, cooking for him and caring for him just as she would her own father. He called her Daughter. She couldn't let Toma kill him. But if Elaak won the fight with Winsit, he would eat Winsit's heart, and the evil in him would grow even stronger. They would be in grave danger.

"Help me," she prayed, and because she was so brave and because her heart was full of love, the great spirit Glooscap came to her in the form of a jay.

"Look at the ground by your feet," the bird told her. Nesoowa looked and saw some bright red flowers growing there, flowers she had never seen before.

"If Elaak wins the battle, crush the blossoms of these flowers with water and give them to him to drink." Then the bird flew away.

"Hurry!" Toma shouted. "Winsit is coming!"

Nesoowa grabbed a handful of the red flowers and ran toward the cave. She and her husband stopped up their ears with moss and held each other as the ground began to shake beneath them. Soon their ears started burning as the air was filled with the horrible war cries of the Chenoos.

For a long time they stayed in the cave and waited. They could still feel the ground shaking as Elaak and Winsit hurled boulders and trees at each other and wrestled each other to the ground.

Finally it grew quiet and calm. "I'm going out," Toma said. Nesoowa followed him.

There on the ground near the cave lay the two Chenoos, locked in an embrace of death. Winsit was on top of Elaak, his hands circling his enemy's throat. Elaak continued to pitch his head and twist his body back and forth, but slowly and surely Winsit was managing to squeeze all the life out of him.

Elaak twisted again, trying to free himself. "Help me," he gasped.

"Help you?" Winsit laughed, rolling his red eyes back into his head. "Who would help you, crazy old man?"

With a cry, Toma threw himself onto the Chenoo's shoulders and plunged the golden horn into Winsit's ear. Within seconds, Winsit was dead.

Elaak twisted himself out from beneath the dead Chenoo's body. The rage of battle was still coursing through him, so that he couldn't even see Nesoowa and Toma standing far below him on the ground. He flung his arms high in victory. "Now I will eat his heart!" he cried in delight.

But Nesoowa was ready. In her hands she held a cup of water mixed with the blossoms of the magic plant. Bravely she climbed onto Winsit's body and looked up into Elaak's eyes. "Wait, Father!" she called. "Before you eat his heart, drink this to celebrate."

Elaak paused. As if a spell had come over him, he reached down and took the cup from her hands, drinking it down with one swallow.

In the same moment, he began to shrink. Soon he was the size of a man once more. His expression changed. His eyes became soft and clear; his shoulders sagged. All the rage and hatred of the Chenoo drained out of him. He became just an ordinary, tired old man.

Elaak held out his hand to Nesoowa. "Take me home, my daughter," he said with a sad, gentle smile.

CLEVER MARCELA

arcela was working in her father's pumpkin patch, looking pretty as a pumpkin herself, when the king rode by on his fine white horse, hunting for wild pigs.

"Hey, girl," he called to Marcela, "get me some water to drink, and be quick about it. Can't you see I'm thirsty?"

"Hey, king," Marcela called back, "you're so grand and we're so poor. We haven't any cup good enough for *you* to drink from, I'm sure. If we had a cup of gold, well, then I'd gladly bring you some water."

"Never mind the cup," the king replied, smiling, for he thought he'd never seen a girl so pretty as this poor peasant's daughter. "Just bring me some water, and if it's cool and clean, that's good enough for me."

So Marcela brought the king some water in a clay cup her mother had made. After the king had drunk from it, she looked him straight in the eye and threw the cup hard against the wall of her father's cottage, shattering it into a thousand pieces.

The king was shocked. "Now, why did you do that?" he cried angrily. "You know I'm of royal blood, the king of this country, and you are nothing but a poor peasant girl. Who are you, to act so proud?"

Marcela curtsied sweetly and lowered her eyes. "Oh, my king, I broke the cup, made for me by my dear dead mother so long ago, because now that you have drunk from it, I wouldn't want it to be used by another."

The king could think of nothing to say to this. As a matter of fact, he looked quite flattered. He just smiled at Marcela and went quietly on his way.

Back at his palace, he found he couldn't stop thinking about Marcela and her saucy smile and pretty eyes. He'd been looking all over the kingdom for the girl clever enough to be his bride, and now perhaps he'd found her. As a test, he sent one of his soldiers back to Marcela's pumpkin patch. "Give her this large round bottle, which has such a very small neck. Tell the girl to put one of her pumpkins inside, without breaking the bottle, and send it back to me."

When the soldier came to Marcela's cottage, he found her sitting outside, sorting seeds and telling stories to entertain her old father. The soldier presented the king's bottle to Marcela and ordered her to put a whole pumpkin inside without breaking the bottle.

Marcela's father trembled with fear. "Dear Daughter, what kind of a request is this? Not even a sorcerer could fit a pumpkin into a bottle with such a narrow neck. Now the king will surely have us thrown into prison."

But Marcela only laughed. "Don't worry, Father. I know how to please this king of ours." She sent the soldier back to the palace, telling him she didn't have any pumpkins fine enough for the king at present, but as soon as she did, her father would bring one straight to the palace.

Then she planted a pumpkin seed inside the bottle. Each day she watered the seed. She let it sit in the sunniest spots of the garden and sang songs to it, until soon the pumpkin plant produced the finest little pumpkin ever seen, sitting snugly inside the king's bottle.

"My pumpkin is ready," she said to her father. "Take it to the palace tomorrow. And when you see the king, tell him to take out the pumpkin without breaking the bottle and send the bottle home with you, so I may grow him another."

Marcela's father went off to the palace and delivered the pumpkin to the king, along with his daughter's message.

When the king saw the pumpkin in the bottle and heard her request, he was sure Marcela must be as clever as she was pretty. Of course he couldn't take the pumpkin out of the bottle. She was just trying to trick him. He decided to see if he could outwit her in return.

"Tell your daughter I thank her very much, but I have no use for another pumpkin. Instead of the bottle, I'm sending her this sheep. She must sell the sheep for six pieces of silver and send me back the money — but it must be carried back to me on this very same sheep."

Marcela's father brought the sheep home to his daughter, worrying all the way that the king would throw them into prison, for surely his daughter would never be able to sell the sheep and still send it back to the king alive — it was impossible!

When Marcela saw the sheep and heard the message, she laughed. "You know, Father," she said, "this king of ours is quite a clever man. He's almost as clever as I am, and he's handsome as well. I just might have to marry him."

Her father begged her to mind her tongue, but Marcela only tossed her head and led the sheep off to the fields. There she sheared off all its wool. Then she wove the wool into a fine piece of cloth, which she took to market and sold for six silver pieces. The next day Marcela's father carried the sheep back to the king's palace, the money tied to its neck with a handkerchief.

When the king saw that Marcela had again proved more clever than he, he became a little irritated. Trying once more to outwit her, he sent her a tiny bird, ordering her to make him seven dinners from it.

Marcela listened to the king's message, looked at the tiny bird, which couldn't possibly make even one dinner, and thought for five minutes. Then she pulled a pin out of her skirt and handed it to her father. "Give this to the king, Father dear. Ask him to make me a steel frying pan, a knife, and a spit out of it, so that I can cook him the bird properly."

This time the king was forced to admit that he would never outwit the peasant's clever daughter. He threw up his hands. "In all the kingdom, there's no one as clever as your daughter, old man. I think I'll have to marry her."

The next day Marcela came to the palace, and she and the king were married in a grand ceremony that lasted seven days and seven nights. When the wedding was over, however, the king had a serious talk with his new queen.

"Now, my dear, I know you are very clever, but I don't want you meddling in my affairs," he said. "I'm the king, after all, and if I ever hear you've interfered with my decisions, I'll send you right back to the pumpkin patch."

Marcela swore she had no interest in trying to run affairs of state. "After all, I'm just a poor peasant girl, and you are the king, my lord," she said. But the king looked at her with suspicion, for he knew well enough that she was just as able to run the kingdom as he.

To please her husband, Marcela kept her word and didn't try to meddle in the king's business. But one day two men came before the king, begging him to settle their dispute. One man owned a mare, who had foaled in the marketplace. The colt ran under a wagon, and the owner of the wagon was now claiming the colt as his property.

The king, who wasn't really listening to the story, carelessly pronounced, "The man who owns the wagon is, of course, the owner of the colt."

When Marcela heard of the king's foolish decision, she decided she needed to teach him a lesson in good judgment. She called for the man who had lost the case and whispered a plan to help him win his colt back. "But remember," she warned in parting, "you mustn't tell the king who gave you this advice."

That afternoon the king went riding out to hunt. Before he had traveled far, however, his horse became tangled up in a fishnet spread across the dusty road.

"What in the world are you doing with a fishnet spread across the road?" he asked the man standing by the net.

"I'm trying to catch fish, my king," the man replied.

"And how do you expect to catch fish in the middle of the road?"

"Well, sire, it's as easy for me to catch fish in the road as it is for a wagon to give birth to a colt" was the man's answer.

The king recognized the fisherman as the plaintiff who had come before him that very morning, and he realized he had made a poor decision in the case. He promised the man he would have his colt returned to him. But the king also knew that Marcela must be at the bottom of this, for only his wife was clever enough to think of such a witty plan. He rode straight back to the palace, growing angrier and angrier as he thought of his wife's disobedience.

"You promised me you wouldn't interfere in affairs of state, and now you have broken your promise," he fumed. "Get out of my house. Take whatever you want in the palace — gold, jewels, whatever pleases you. Just get out of my sight. Our marriage is finished."

"Very well, my lord," said Marcela, bowing her head sadly. "I will be gone by morning."

That evening Marcela cooked the king a delicious meal, seasoning it with plenty of salt. She served him his dinner with two bottles of wine, and the salt made the king so thirsty that he drank up all the wine and soon fell into a deep and dreamless sleep. As he slept, Marcela bundled him into a cart and pushed him to her father's house.

The king woke the next morning to find himself in Marcela's father's little cottage, surrounded by the pumpkin patch. Of course he was very surprised. "Marcela, what is the meaning of this?" he cried.

Marcela kissed him soundly. "Well, dearest king," she said with a smile, "you told me to take whatever I wanted from the palace, and I wanted you. I hope you don't mind too much."

The king realized that once again, his clever wife had outwitted him. He took Marcela and her father back to the palace, and he decreed that from that time forth Marcela should be chief justice and decide all court cases. This she agreed to, and everyone lived well and happily all the rest of their days.

SISTER LACE

 any years ago there lived a woman who was very talented at making lace, so everyone called her Sister Lace. She created lacework plants and birds and animals so beautiful and intricate that they seemed to be living creatures. Her work was the greatest treasure of her village, and anyone who owned a veil or curtain or dress or jacket made by Sister Lace was considered very lucky indeed.

Word of Sister Lace's skill spread throughout the land, and girls from all over the country came to study with her. Sometimes her students would become frustrated and despair of ever being able to make lace as beautiful as hers. But Sister Lace was a kind and patient teacher. "Do not worry," she told the girls. "Everything I know, someday you will know, too. You must learn to make lace with your heart as well as your fingers. That is the secret. In time you will learn how to do it."

One day a peddler came to the court of the emperor and sold him a handkerchief made by Sister Lace. The work was so exquisite that the emperor insisted on finding out who had made it. When he heard about Sister Lace, he became angry with his courtiers. "Why didn't you tell me there was a woman of such skill living in my kingdom?" he scolded them. "She should be here at court working for me. Lace this fine should be made only for the emperor." Then he sent out a contingent of soldiers to bring Sister Lace to the palace at once.

When the soldiers arrived at Sister Lace's cottage, she refused to go with them. "I have no interest in the emperor," she declared. "My work is here in my village, making lace for

THE SERPENT SLAYER

my people and sharing my skill with the girls who come to study with me. I cannot leave them."

"How dare you refuse to see the emperor!" one of the soldiers shouted. The girls gathered around their teacher, trying to protect her, but the soldiers knocked them down and seized Sister Lace. As she was carried away, she called back to her students, "Be strong; be patient. Remember everything I've taught you, and someday you'll make lace finer than my own — I swear it."

At the emperor's palace, Sister Lace refused to walk and was dragged before the emperor. "Stop this nonsense, woman," the emperor commanded. "You are here now, and you will never go back to your village. You will marry me, and from this time forward, you will make lace only for me."

Sister Lace thought of the good people of her village, her beautiful cottage where she had spent such happy years working at her craft, and the girls who came to study with her. She hated the emperor with all her heart. When he tried to draw her close to him, she scratched at his eyes and kicked at him. "I'll never marry you!" she cried.

The emperor's face grew red with anger and embarrassment. No woman had ever treated him like this before. He pushed her away and ordered his guards to throw her into prison.

The next day the emperor came to stand by the door of her prison cell. Sister Lace sat on the bare floor, staring sadly at her empty hands. She didn't even notice him. The powerful ruler rattled the bars of her cell to get her attention. "Foolish woman! If you marry me, you will live in comfort all the rest of your days. All you will have to do is open your mouth to be fed and hold out your hands to be dressed," he told her.

Sister Lace raised her head and looked into the emperor's eyes. "I know how to feed myself and dress myself. Why should I marry you? I don't love you. I love no one but the people of my village and the girls who come to study with me. I love nothing but making lace. I want nothing from you."

The emperor laughed angrily. "Very well," he said. "If you love making lace so much, make me a live rooster on a length of lace. Then you can return to your stupid village. Otherwise, you will stay here forever. You have seven days."

The prison guards brought material to her jail cell, and for seven days Sister Lace worked day and night to make a rooster. On the seventh day it was done. She pricked her finger with her needle and rubbed the blood on the rooster's feathers, and a tear rolled down her cheek and fell into the rooster's mouth like a pearl. With a flap of its wings, the rooster stood up and crowed.

Soon the emperor and his courtiers came to the prison cell. The emperor was shocked to find a live rooster struggling to break free of a length of lace. "What kind of trick is this?" he cried. "You didn't make this rooster. It's one of the birds from the palace. Make

26

me a wild partridge. I'll give you another seven days to finish it, and if you can't do it, you'll be my wife."

As he turned to leave, the rooster suddenly broke free of the length of lace, flew at the emperor, and began tearing at his forehead with its claws. "Free Sister Lace!" the rooster crowed. "Free Sister Lace or it will be the death of you!"

The courtiers quickly caught the rooster and killed it. The emperor's eyes grew cold as ice, and his mouth set in a grim line. "I will never let her go," he muttered as he walked away, wiping the blood from his temples.

Sister Lace worked day and night to make the wild partridge. On the seventh day it was finished. She pricked her finger with her needle and brushed the blood onto the partridge's feathers. She thought of her village, and a tear rolled down her cheek and dropped into the partridge's mouth like a pearl. With a flap of its wings, the partridge stood up and ran about the prison cell in circles.

When the emperor came once again to see his prisoner, he found a live partridge perched on a nest of lace in the corner of her cell.

"Where did this bird come from?" he shouted. "I never told you to make me a partridge. I told you to make me a heavenly dragon. Enough of this nonsense. Make me a dragon within seven days, or you'll never see your home again."

As the emperor turned to leave the cell, the partridge flew from the corner and landed on his head, scratching at his neck with its claws. "Free Sister Lace!" the partridge called. "Free Sister Lace or it will be the death of you!"

The courtiers hurried to chase the partridge from the emperor's head, beating it with sticks until it was dead. The emperor left the prison with blood dripping down his neck and the bitter taste of anger on his tongue.

For seven days and seven nights, Sister Lace worked in her prison cell, though her eyes were burning from tears and exhaustion and her fingers were sore and clumsy. She ignored the pain and worked with her heart, and on the seventh day she had finished the dragon. She knew it was more beautiful than anything she had ever made before. She pricked her finger and brushed the blood along the dragon's scales, painting it red, and a tear rolled down her cheek and dropped into the dragon's mouth like a pearl. With a toss of its fiery head, the dragon came alive.

Sister Lace held the little dragon on her lap and wept. "Oh, my little dragon, you are more beautiful than anything I have ever made, but what good will it do me?" she cried. "Now the emperor will tell me he wanted a fish instead of a dragon, and he will kill us both. I know I'll never be able to go back to my village again."

Soon the emperor came yet again to the door of her prison cell. When he saw the dragon with its lacy scales, he began to tremble. "This is not a dragon — it's a snake!" he shouted, backing away from Sister Lace.

The little dragon erupted in fury. It raised its head and breathed out a stream of fire, which curled around the emperor and burned him to death. Soon the prison was on fire, and then all the palace was burning up in a roaring blaze.

Riding on the back of the dragon, Sister Lace flew into the sky. There she has worked, from that day to this, making the lace that covers the night sky with stars.

The girls of her country have never forgotten Sister Lace's promise that someday they will be able to make lace as fine as hers. Whenever they look up at the evening sky, they remember her secret, and their lace is as beautiful as the stars.

THE REBEL PRINCESS

There was once a great emperor who did not have any children. There was also a king who was childless. Both the king and the emperor wandered the world over, seeking a remedy.

After months of traveling, they happened to arrive on the same day in a large city, where they spent the night at the same inn. Recognizing each other as men of royal bearing, they decided to dine together that evening. After sharing several bottles of wine, and discussing at great length the business of kingship, they discovered that they were both traveling for the same reason. And they vowed that if, after they returned home, their wives gave birth to children, and one child should be a girl and the other a boy, they would arrange a marriage between the two.

Soon the emperor and the king returned to their wives, and within the year they had both become fathers. The king's wife gave birth to a son, called Zev. The emperor's wife had a daughter, named Judith. But as so often happens, now that the emperor had what he'd wanted, he forgot the promise he'd made to the king and never once considered betrothing his daughter to the king's son.

The children grew to be fine young people, as clever and kind and courageous as any parent could hope for. When they were old enough, their parents sent them abroad to study, and it happened that both came under the guidance of a famous scholar.

Judith and Zev were by far the most brilliant students among all those who studied with the sage, and they soon became fast friends. They spent countless hours poring over ancient manuscripts, discussing the meaning of life, and sharing their hopes and dreams for the future.

The prince and princess studied with their teacher for three years, and the days passed quickly. When at last it came time for them to return to their separate kingdoms, Judith and Zev realized that they loved each other and could not bear the thought of separation.

"Here is a plan," Judith told Zev. "You are a prince and I'm a princess and we must marry someone. Let us pledge to marry each other. When we return home we will tell our parents of our engagement. Then they can arrange the rest."

The prince and princess parted tearfully, but were confident that it would not be long before they were reunited.

When Judith arrived at her father's palace, she was welcomed with great joy. But when she told her father about the prince, and asked him to arrange their wedding, he became troubled and fell silent. While she had been gone, her father had promised her to the son of a rich and powerful lord.

Knowing what a determined young woman his daughter could be, the emperor was afraid to tell her what he had done. Instead, he decided to wait, hoping his daughter would forget her infatuation with the faraway prince once she had settled back into life at home.

Meanwhile, Zev's father sent many letters to Judith's father, reminding him of their pact to each other and inquiring about plans for the wedding. But the emperor let the letters go unanswered. He even hid the ones that the prince sent to Judith. As the months went by, Zev began to fear somehow that his letters were not reaching their destination. He knew he must visit the emperor in person.

When Prince Zev arrived at the palace, the emperor greeted him politely. But he also gave secret orders that the prince was not to be allowed to see the princess, and that she was not to be told of his visit. The prince was introduced to dignitaries, taken out on hunting parties, and shown all the interesting sights of the kingdom. But every time he asked to see Judith, or tried to make plans for their engagement, the emperor would change the subject or admonish him to have patience.

Then one day, as the prince was walking through the palace gardens, he found the princess reading a book under an apple tree. The young lovers were overjoyed to see each other again.

"But what has taken you so long?" Judith cried. "I've been waiting for months without any word from you!"

When Zev explained that he had been writing to her faithfully and had already been in the palace for several weeks, Judith instantly understood the situation.

"It must be that my father has betrothed me to some other prince and is trying to discourage you without actually refusing you," she said. "We have no time to waste — we must run away together. Once we are actually married, there is nothing my father can do."

The lovers met at the palace gates before dawn and ran down to the harbor. They set sail on the prince's ship before anyone knew they were gone.

They sailed together for many days, then docked the ship at a deserted island to search for fresh supplies. Zev decided to hunt for wild animals in the forest, while Judith chose to stay on the beach to collect coconuts.

Soon Judith had gathered all the coconuts they needed, but Zev did not return. The princess grew worried and decided to go look for him. After wandering for many hours without finding any trace of her prince, she circled back to the beach and climbed a tall coconut tree, hoping that she would be able to catch sight of him from its height.

It so happened that at that very moment the son of a wealthy merchant was sailing by the island in a ship filled with valuable goods. Looking through his telescope, he was astonished to see a beautiful woman sitting at the top of a coconut tree. He ordered his sailors to dock the ship, and he and his men set out to capture the lovely girl.

When the merchant's son came to the coconut tree, the princess refused to come down, or even to speak to him. But when he ordered his men to chop down the tree, Judith agreed to go to his ship, but only if he promised not to marry her until they reached his home port.

The merchant's son was smitten by the beautiful princess and happily agreed to her request. They left the island and sailed straight to his father's city.

Upon their arrival, Judith told the merchant's son that he must first go announce her to his family so they could come to the harbor and welcome her as his future bride. The lovesick young man immediately obeyed and hurried home to speak to his parents.

After the merchant's son had gone, the princess gave all of the sailors wine to drink, insisting that they celebrate the forthcoming wedding. Before long, they were all drunk, and they left the ship to go into the city. As soon as Judith was alone, she hauled up the ship's anchor, unfurled the sails, and set out to sea.

When the wealthy merchant's family went to the harbor to meet the bride-to-be, the ship was gone, along with all its cargo. The merchant was furious with his foolish son and banished him from his household. The unfortunate young man was forced to become a beggar.

Judith sailed the ship toward the island where she'd last seen Zev. But a terrible storm blew her far off course, and the ship washed up on the shores of a distant land. The king of this country came to the harbor to investigate the fine ship, sailed single-handedly by a mysterious young woman.

As soon as the king laid eyes on the princess, he fell madly in love and insisted that she marry him. Judith agreed, on the condition that the ship's cargo remain in its hold, so that on the day of the wedding she could unload it and show the people the great riches she was bringing to their country.

The king, dazzled by Judith's beauty, charm, and independence, agreed to everything she asked. He also sent the daughters of the eleven most powerful lords in the kingdom to be her ladies-in-waiting. The women passed the time playing music, writing poems, and telling stories. The ladies-in-waiting loved to hear about Judith's adventures on the high seas, and how she had sailed her ship alone through the terrible storm.

On the day before the wedding, the princess took all the ladies on board the ship so they might see it for themselves. Then she confessed that although she was to be married to the king, she was already in love with another. She told them how she had lost her beloved Zev, and the eleven ladies-in-waiting all agreed that they would like nothing better than to help Judith find her true love. As soon as night had fallen, they untied the moorings and set sail.

By the time the king discovered the ship was missing, and with it his bride-to-be, not to mention eleven daughters of the most powerful lords in his kingdom, there was nothing to be done. In anger, the fathers of the ladies-in-waiting dethroned the king and banished him from the kingdom.

Meanwhile, Judith and the eleven ladies sailed in search of Zev until they ran out of food and came to an island. They landed, only to find it was ruled by a band of blood-thirsty pirates. The pirates seized the ship and took the women as prisoners.

Before they could be killed, Judith, thinking quickly, said to the chieftain, "We, too, are pirates, but you are pirates of strength, while we are pirates of cleverness. Why doesn't each of you take one of us for a wife? Then we can use our cleverness to help you increase your wealth."

The pirates agreed this was an excellent idea and prepared a great feast to celebrate the weddings. The princess and her ladies brought out many casks of wine from their ship, and the pirates drank and drank until they fell asleep. While the pirates were sleeping, Judith and her ladies threw them overboard and they drowned. Then the women explored the island, and found a cave full of treasure, with more gold and jewels than any of them had ever seen. They loaded the treasure onto their ship, and once more set sail.

Now the ladies disguised themselves as pirates, and sailed the open sea for many weeks until they spied another ship on the horizon. Hoping that the other sailors could help her find Zev, the princess turned her ship in that direction.

On the other ship was a young king, out for a day's excursion. When the young king saw the princess's ship approaching, he decided to climb the tall mast to get a better look. But the sun's glare off the water blinded him, and he lost his grasp and fell overboard. Judith saw what happened and immediately dove into the water, hoping to rescue the drowning king. But she was too late, and the best she could do was bring his body back to his ship. The distraught crew insisted that Judith and her sailors, still disguised as men, return with them to their city.

When the counselors and noblemen of the city met the ship's captain, they were deeply impressed by his wisdom and courage, as well as the great wealth he carried on his ship. After the young king's funeral, they asked Judith to become the new king. Of course they didn't suspect that the brave captain was really an emperor's daughter disguised as a man!

So the princess became king of that country, and she appointed her ladies-in-waiting as ministers. As king, she ordered that the finest sculptor in the land create a statue of her, which was placed at the gates of the city. She then instructed soldiers to stand by the statue day and night and arrest anyone who wept upon seeing the statue's face.

It happened that three people were arrested and brought before the new king. The first was Prince Zev, who had been searching for Judith ever since the merchant's son had seized her from the deserted island. The second was the merchant's son himself, and the third was the king who had been banished from his country when the princess escaped with the eleven ladies. All three men had been roaming the world, living from hand to mouth. When they had seen the statue of the new king, they had instantly recognized the features of the princess and were unable to conceal their distress.

When the princess had heard their stories, she turned first to the deposed king.

"Your countrymen banished you because of the eleven ladies who pledged themselves to my cause. If they choose, they may now return with you to their families. Your people will be delighted, and they will reinstate you."

The ladies, who were happy to return to their own country, agreed to leave with the king. The princess then turned to the merchant's son. "Your father banished you because you had lost your ship and its goods," she said. "Go to the harbor. Your ship is waiting for you there, filled with cargo a hundred times more valuable than what you lost."

Finally, the princess turned to the prince. "While you have been searching for me, I, too, have been searching for you. Come, my love, let us go home."

Then she revealed to the court that she was actually a woman, and told them the story of how she had come to be sailing the seas so close to their kingdom.

Judith and Zev returned to her father the emperor, who welcomed them with open arms. They were married at last, in a great celebration, and lived happily together for the rest of their days.

BEEBYEEBYEE AND THE WATER GOD

nce there was a chief who had many, many wives, and each of his wives had children. He was a lucky man, because all of his children were well behaved. All, that is, except one, and her name was Beebyeebyee.

Beebyeebyee was very stubborn. She never wanted to go to the farm with her sisters. She never wanted to help her mother pound corn *fufu* or help with the washing, and she always wanted fish and meat to eat. Every day her mother said to her, "Beebyeebyee, you're a bad girl. You're lazy and disobedient, and I'll never be able to find a husband for you."

But Beebyeebyee would just shrug. "Then I'll find my own husband," she answered each time.

Now, Beebyeebyee's village was near the river, and all of Beebyeebyee's brothers were fishermen. Every day her brothers brought fish home to their mother, and she cooked it for them. The frying fish smelled so good, it made Beebyeebyee's mouth water. But whenever she asked her mother to give her some, her mother would just laugh at her.

"Why should I give fish to a little girl like you? If you want some fish, go catch your own," she scolded.

One day Beebyeebyee got tired of hearing this. "All right, I *will* go catch some of my own," she said. She went to her canoe and paddled far down the river, looking for a good place to start fishing. At last she came to a sandy island and pulled her boat onto the beach to rest for a bit. As she was relaxing on the sand, she saw someone coming out of the river. She was frightened because it was a water god. She could tell because although he came out of the water, he wasn't wet at all.

"Hello, Beebyeebyee," the water god greeted her. Beebyeebyee stopped being frightened, for he sounded nice. Besides, he was extremely handsome.

"What do you want?" she asked him.

"I want you to marry me," he said. Beebyeebyee thought about it for a while, and finally she decided this was a good idea. So Beebyeebyee and the water god got married then and there. Then he asked her why she had come out to this island, and Beebyeebyee told him how her mother and brothers never gave her any fish.

"They were very selfish," the water god cried. "I'll give you plenty of fish." With those words he dove into the water, and he soon came back with so many fish that they filled Beebyeebyee's entire boat, until there was hardly room for her to sit down.

Before Beebyeebyee left that day, the water god taught her a song. "If ever you want more fish," he said, "just come to this spot and sing:

> *Ayun jimi jolo*
>
> *Ayun jimi jolo*
>
> *Ayun jimi jolo*
>
> Beebyeebyee
>
> *Bena bela jimi jolo*
>
> *Bena bela jimi jolo.*

Then I'll come to see you."

When Beebyeebyee got back to her village, everyone was very surprised to see how many fish she had. There was enough for everyone in the village. Beebyeebyee gave all her fish away, and no one went to bed hungry that night.

The next day, the girl set out again for the little island in the river. When she arrived, she sang:

> *"Ayun jimi jolo*
>
> *Ayun jimi jolo*
>
> *Ayun jimi jolo*
>
> Beebyeebyee
>
> *Bena bela jimi jolo*
>
> *Bena bela jimi jolo."*

Her husband the water god came out of the river, and he and his wife spent the whole day playing on the sandy beach. When it came time for Beebyeebyee to go back home, the water god filled her boat with fish again. Beebyeebyee went home and shared her fish with the rest of the village.

For many months, this continued. Almost every day Beebyeebyee set out in her canoe and paddled to the island to meet her husband. They passed the days together happily,

and when it came time for Beebyeebyee to go home at night, the water god filled her boat with enough fish to feed the whole village.

You would think the villagers would be happy to have Beebyeebyee bring them fish every day. But all the experienced fishermen, who were used to being the most important people in the village, became jealous of Beebyeebyee. They couldn't understand how this young girl could get so many fish, while they worked hard all day and couldn't catch half as much as she brought home.

"She must be using magic," the fishermen grumbled. "Nobody can catch that many fish without magic."

"She's a bad witch," some of the young men said. "She'll bring ruin on us all." You see, they were worried, because now that everyone had enough fish to eat, no one gave the fishermen the same respect anymore. So the men started whispering bad things about Beebyeebyee, and soon everyone had heard the rumors.

One day some of the young men decided to follow Beebyeebyee and see where she was getting all her fish. While she paddled her canoe down the river, they walked quietly on the bank far enough away so that she couldn't see them. After she came to the island, they hid behind some bushes and watched her. She sang the song to call her husband:

"Ayun jimi jolo
Ayun jimi jolo
Ayun jimi jolo
Beebyeebyee
Bena bela jimi jolo
Bena bela jimi jolo."

Then the water god came out of the river. The young men hiding behind the bushes saw everything. They saw the water god give Beebyeebyee all her fish. When they got back to the village, they told everybody, "Beebyeebyee is meeting a terrible monster on the island in the river. He's the one who gives her all the fish. He probably wants to make us all fat so he can come and eat us." Now everyone thought Beebyeebyee was bad, and they stopped trusting her. But they didn't tell her anything.

The next day Beebyeebyee couldn't go fishing because it was time to harvest the yams and she had to go and work in her yam field. After she left, the young men stole her canoe and quickly paddled to the island. One of the men sang in a high voice that sounded just like Beebyeebyee's:

"Ayun jimi jolo
Ayun jimi jolo
Ayun jimi jolo
Beebyeebyee

Bena bela jimi jolo
Bena bela jimi jolo."

Soon the water god came out of the river, thinking Beebyeebyee was calling him. As soon as he came out, the young men seized him and killed him. Then they threw his body in the bushes.

The young fishermen went back to the village and told the people that they had killed the terrible water monster. They told everyone except Beebyeebyee. The villagers were happy and laughed to think how the fishermen had tricked Beebyeebyee.

After a few days, Beebyeebyee decided to visit her husband again. She paddled her canoe down the river to the island. Soon she was singing:

"Ayun jimi jolo
Ayun jimi jolo
Ayun jimi jolo
Beebyeebyee
Bena bela jimi jolo
Bena bela jimi jolo."

She sang her song twice, but the water god didn't come out of the river. She sang and sang until she was hoarse, but still he didn't come. Beebyeebyee sat crying and crying on the sandy beach. She cried so much that finally the water god's brother came out of the river and talked to her. He told her how the young men had killed her husband. "Don't worry," he told her. "The people of your village will pay for what they did to my brother." Then he loaded her boat with fish.

Beebyeebyee went back home and shared her catch as she had always done. The people of the village took their fish, but that was the last time. In the night the river rose and flooded every house in the village except for Beebyeebyee's.

KATE CRACKERNUTS

 nce upon a time, there was a king who had a daughter named Anne. His first wife died, so he married another, who already had a daughter named Kate. The two girls loved each other even more than sisters, but the queen was jealous because the king's daughter was prettier than her own. She asked the henwife to give her a charm to spoil the looks of the king's daughter. The henwife told her to send the girl to her and to make sure that she didn't eat anything beforehand.

The next morning, bright and early, the queen sent Anne to the henwife, telling her to fetch some eggs. Anne went as she was told, but before she left, she grabbed a crust of bread from the pantry to eat along the way. When she came to the henwife's, the henwife told her to lift the lid off the pot that was bubbling on the fire. Anne did as she was told, but nothing happened. The henwife sent her home with the eggs. "Tell your stepmother to mind her pantry door," the henwife said.

Anne went home and told the queen what the henwife had said, so the queen knew that Anne had found something to eat before she left and the charm couldn't work. The next day the queen made sure to lock the pantry door, then sent her stepdaughter off to the henwife's, the same as before. But this morning a farmer gave Anne a handful of peas when she passed by him on the road, and again the charm didn't work.

The third morning, the queen went along with the girl to the henwife's and made sure she didn't eat so much as a crumb before they got there. This time, when Anne lifted the lid off the henwife's pot, her own pretty head fell off, and a sheep's head jumped out of the pot to take its place.

The queen took the king's daughter back to the castle, satisfied. But when Kate saw what had happened to Anne, it broke her heart. She wrapped a fine linen cloth around her sister's head and took her hand, and together they left the castle and set off to seek their fortunes.

They walked for days and they walked for weeks, farther than anyone can say, until at last they came to a king's castle. Kate knocked at the door and asked if she and her sister could pass the night there. It turned out that this king had a son who was wasting away from a mysterious illness. No one knew what his trouble was, but every night the prince grew weaker and weaker. The king had promised a bag of silver to anyone who could sit with his son till morning came and find out what was sickening him.

Right away, Kate said that she would sit with the prince that night. She hid herself behind the door, in a place where she could see the prince sleeping but he couldn't see her, and she waited. Until midnight all went well, but when the clock struck twelve, the prince rose, dressed himself, and slipped downstairs. Quiet as a mouse, Kate followed him.

The prince went to the stable, saddled his horse, and called for his hound. As he leapt to the saddle, Kate leapt lightly up behind him — so lightly he didn't even notice she was there. Together they rode through the greenwood, and as they rode, Kate plucked nuts from the trees and filled her apron with them. They rode on and on until they came to a green hill. The prince drew up his horse and said, "Open, open, open, and let in the prince with his horse and his hound."

"And his lady behind him," added Kate very softly. A door appeared in the side of the green hill. Silently it swung open, and Kate and the prince passed through. They rode into a magnificent hall, lit bright as day by the fire of ten thousand candles. As soon as the prince came into the hall, many beautiful fairy women dressed in ball gowns of satin and velvet surrounded him and led him off to dance.

Unnoticed, Kate slid quietly into the shadows and seated herself by the door. There she watched the prince, who danced and danced until he could dance no more. Finally he fell to the floor with exhaustion, and the fairy women fanned him and gave him wine to drink, until he staggered to his feet again and continued dancing. So it went until at last the cock crowed to greet the dawn. Then the prince called for his horse. Kate jumped up lightly behind him again, and together they rode back through the greenwood. When the morning sun rose, the king and queen came in and found the prince asleep in his bed and Kate quietly cracking nuts by the fire.

Kate told them that the prince had had a good night. She agreed to sit up with him another night, but this time only if the king gave her a bag of gold.

The second night passed as the first. The prince woke up at midnight and rode away to the green hill, with Kate riding behind him, plucking nuts from the trees and putting

them in her apron. When he came into the great hall, the fairy women surrounded him as before and led him away to dance, while Kate hid herself by the door. From there she watched two little fairy babies, who were playing on the floor with a golden wand.

After a time, Kate heard some of the women talking. "If only Kate Crackernuts knew that three strokes of that wand would make her sick sister as pretty as she ever was," said one of the fairies to the others.

Kate waited until the fairy women went back to the dance. Then she began to roll her nuts across the floor toward the babies. The babies grew interested in the nuts. They forgot about playing with the wand and left it lying in the corner. Kate snatched it up and put it in her apron.

The cock crowed. The prince called for his horse and hound, and Kate leapt up behind him. Together they rode home to the castle, where the prince went back to bed. Kate ran right away to her sister's room and touched Anne's head three times with the fairy wand. The ugly sheep's head rolled right off, and Anne's pretty head reappeared in its place. So Kate went back to the prince's room and sat by the fire, cracking her nuts and eating them.

In the morning Kate told everyone that the prince had had a good night. She agreed to watch him a third night, but this time only if she could marry him. The king and queen agreed, and for the third time, Kate rode with the prince to the green hill, gathering nuts from the trees and putting them in her apron.

That night while the prince was dancing, Kate watched the fairy babies playing with a little birdie. By and by, she heard one of the fairy women say, "If only Kate Crackernuts knew that three bites of that birdie would make the prince well again."

Kate rolled all the nuts in her apron toward the fairy babies, and at last they forgot about the birdie and came to play with the nuts. Kate put the birdie in her pocket and waited for the prince until it was time to go back home.

When they got back to the castle, Kate plucked the birdie's feathers and cooked it over the fire. Soon the prince woke up and smelled the birdie cooking. "Oh," he said. "I wish I had a bite of that birdie!"

Kate gave him a bite, and as soon as he'd swallowed, some color came back into his cheeks. "If only I had another bite of that birdie!" the prince sighed again.

When Kate gave him a second bite, the prince sat right up in bed, and his eyes grew bright. "Oh, I do wish I had a third bite of that birdie," he said, strong and clear. So Kate gave him a third bite, and he rose, quite well, and dressed himself. When the king and queen came in that morning, they found Kate and the prince sitting happily by the fire, cracking nuts together.

So Kate married the prince, and her sister, Anne, married the prince's brother, and they all lived happily and died happily, and that's the end of the story of Kate Crackernuts.

THE OLD WOMAN
AND THE DEVIL

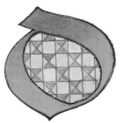nce there was an old woman. Every day she liked to go to the suq and sit on a certain shady patch of grass under a palm tree. Sometimes she would doze off, and other times she would sit and watch the people go by. Everyone in the city knew this was the old woman's place and left her alone.

Then one day the devil came to town. He saw the shady place by the edge of the market and decided that this would be a good spot to start working. That morning when the old woman came hobbling up to the suq, she saw the devil lying under the palm tree in her favorite spot. Well, this old woman had lived a long and difficult life already, and she'd kept worse company than the devil. She figured there was space enough under that palm tree for both of them, so she said good morning and made herself comfortable, just as usual.

For a few hours they got along fine, sitting quietly under the palm tree and gossiping. But when the devil comes to town, he attracts people with evil on their minds. By midmorning the old woman's quiet corner had become the busiest place in the whole market. Before she knew what was happening, thieves and murderers and swindlers and all kinds of wicked people were milling around. It got so noisy, she couldn't think straight, never mind take a nap. People started stepping on her. Someone stole her purse.

So the old woman stood up and went over to the devil and poked him with her stick. "Listen, you," she said to him. "You go find some other place to do your business. This is my spot, and I can't sleep with all this noise. Not only that, but someone just stole my purse."

The devil looked up at her and twirled his mustache. He laughed. "You silly old crone. Don't you know who you're talking to? I'm the devil, and if I decide this is where I want to do business, then this is where I'll do business."

"What's so special about being the devil?" the old woman snorted. "Why, you have no more brains than a chicken, as far as I can see."

Now the devil got so indignant that his horns started to glow. "What do you mean, I've no more brains than a chicken? Who do you think is responsible for all the grief and destruction in this world? Why, just look at all the thieves and murderers, the swindlers and liars and cheaters I've managed to attract in just one morning!"

The old woman snorted again. "Thieves and murderers? You call that a good morning's work? Anyone can attract thieves and murderers. I don't see what's so devilish about that."

"Well, could you do better, old woman?" the devil sputtered.

"I most certainly could."

"That's something I'd like to see," the devil scoffed.

"Very well, you old goat. If you really want to see some devilish work, I'll show you how it's done. But you have to promise that afterward you'll find some other place to do business and leave me alone."

"Ha!" cried the devil. "If you can show me how an old crone like you could be more devilish than the devil himself, I'll take my work elsewhere. But if you can't, you'd do best to watch your tongue and quit your nagging, for things could go worse for you."

"Very well," agreed the old woman. "But remember: once I've proved myself more devilish than you, you must leave me in peace."

She pointed across the square to a prosperous shop, with bolts of colorful cloth from around the world laid out on tables outside the door. "That cloth merchant and his wife have been happily married for well over a year now."

"Yes, I know," said the devil grumpily. "I've managed to stir up trouble in a thousand households around this city, but try as I might, I can't seem to destroy the happiness of that couple."

"Didn't I say you're no brighter than a chicken? Devil or not, you haven't the wits of an old woman. By this evening, that happy couple will be ready for divorce and you will be packing up and moving out of here."

With these words, the old crone stamped off to her house. There she changed her rags for the elegant gown of a rich lady. Then she hurried back to the cloth merchant's shop.

The cloth merchant was delighted to see such a wealthy customer and brought the old woman a glass of mint tea while she carefully inspected all the most expensive silks in the shop.

"No, none of these are quite right," the old woman exclaimed at last. "I need something truly extraordinary. You see, my son has fallen in love with a married woman. It's terrible, but what can I do? He is my only son, the light of my life, and he claims if he can't persuade this woman to leave her husband, he will die of a broken heart. She has agreed to run away with him if he can find her a bolt of cloth more beautiful than any other in this city."

The cloth merchant sympathized with the old woman's problem and went into one of his back rooms where he kept a length of stunningly embroidered silk, imported from the Orient and too fine to put on display with the rest of his merchandise.

"That is just what I've been looking for!" the old woman cried in delight. She paid the cloth merchant a handsome price and hurried off with the package of cloth clutched tightly under her arm.

Then she went straight to the cloth merchant's home and pounded on the door. When his wife appeared, the old woman explained that she was traveling through town and had grown faint from the heat. Could she come in and rest for a few moments, perhaps have a drink of water? The cloth merchant's wife invited her in with a kind smile and begged her to make herself comfortable in the sitting room.

While the wife went off to fetch some cool water from the kitchen, the old woman left her package under one of the low tables in the room, a place where it was sure to be noticed before the end of the day. Then, having thanked the merchant's wife for her hospitality, she continued on her way.

That evening the cloth merchant returned to his home and, as was his custom, went into the sitting room to relax before the call to evening prayer. There he found the package the old woman had left behind and opened it, his hands trembling. Sure enough, it was the very same piece of cloth he'd sold that morning. And what had the old lady said? Her son had fallen in love with a married woman — she must have meant his wife!

Crazy with jealousy, the merchant ran to the kitchen and began to curse at his wife, shouting and throwing all the dishes in the house at her. His wife, convinced her husband had gone mad, ran home to her parents, weeping over her terrible fate.

"Well," said the old woman to the devil, from where they watched just outside the cloth merchant's house, "who has proven to be more devilish today, you or I?"

"You've certainly succeeded where I had failed. They are very unhappy," the devil was forced to admit.

"True. Now you see that an old woman's wits are far superior to those of the devil. But you have only just begun to understand. For while you may be able to bring grief and strife and unhappiness to a home, I am able to bring an unhappy family back together again."

"Ha!" cried the devil. "Are you saying that you could repair the damage all your devilish work has caused today? Never in a million years!"

"Just watch me," the old woman said, laughing.

Bright and early the next morning, she dressed herself once more in the clothes of a rich lady and went back to the cloth merchant's shop.

"Have you any more of that cloth you sold me yesterday?" she asked the merchant. "On my way home from your shop yesterday, I stopped in some kind woman's home for a drink of water, for I was feeling faint from the heat. Foolishly, I forgot my package of cloth at her house, and now I can't remember what the address was."

The merchant listened to her story with amazement. Then he handed her the package of cloth. "It was my house where you stopped, madam, and it was my good wife who offered you the drink of water. How fortunate that your cloth is not lost after all," he said. Then he quickly closed up his shop and hurried to his wife's parents' house to beg forgiveness.

The wife, who truly loved her husband, quickly forgave him and agreed to return home. The devil, admitting defeat, took his business elsewhere and was never seen in that city again. As for the old woman, she has lived in peace from that day to this.

THE MAGIC LAKE

ong ago there was a powerful emperor who lived in a palace of pure gold in the midst of a city more splendid and dazzling than the world had ever known before. Yet for all his wealth and power, the emperor was a sad and anxious old man, for his only son was a sickly child, so weak and tired that he never even left his bed. The aging emperor himself grew sick with worry, wondering what would become of his son — and of his kingdom, should the boy remain too ill to govern.

One night the emperor knelt before his altar fire and prayed with all his heart for the gods to give his son health and strength, to make him a fit ruler for his people. To his amazement, he heard a voice coming from within the fire.

"Let the prince drink water from the magic lake at the end of the world," said the voice, "and he will be well."

Suddenly the fire sputtered and died. A golden flask lay glittering in the ashes.

The emperor was much too old to make the journey to the end of the world himself. So he sent messengers throughout the land, proclaiming that whoever could fill the golden flask with the magic water would be richly rewarded. Many brave men searched everywhere for the magic lake, but not one could find it. The months passed, and still the flask remained empty. Meanwhile, the emperor's son grew weaker with each passing day.

In a valley far from the emperor's palace lived a poor farmer and his wife. They managed to scrape together a meager living by growing corn and potatoes and raising llamas. Their two sons helped to plant and harvest the corn crop, and their little daughter, Sumac, tended their herd of llamas.

It took a long time for word of the emperor's proclamation to reach this distant valley, but when the two brothers finally heard of it, they grew excited at the thought of the emperor's reward.

"Let me and my brother go to search for the magic lake," the elder brother begged his mother and father. "We promise to return in time to help with the harvest."

The farmer and his wife remained silent. They knew it would be a long and dangerous journey to the magic lake, if indeed such a place existed. After all, many brave men had already searched for the lake, but none had managed to find it.

"Think of the reward," the second son cried. "We could be rich!"

"Perhaps it is their destiny to find the lake," the farmer's wife said at last. "In any case, if they wish to try, it is not our place to stand in their way."

"Go if you must," the farmer agreed reluctantly. "But beware of wild beasts and evil spirits."

So the farmer and his wife gave their sons their blessing, and the brothers set out on their journey. But though they traveled far and wide and saw many lakes, none of them was magic.

At last the time came for the crops to be harvested, and the young men knew they must turn back to the farm. But it was hard to give up the dream of the emperor's rich reward.

"I have an idea," said the elder son. "Let's carry a jar of ordinary water to the emperor's palace and say we have brought it from the magic lake. Even if it doesn't cure the prince, the emperor will surely give us a little something for our trouble."

The younger son agreed to the plan, and the next day the two brothers rode straight to the emperor's palace, carrying a jar of plain lake water. They presented the jar to the emperor and his court, saying it was filled with water from the magic lake.

So the emperor called for the golden flask to be brought to him and tried to fill it with water from the brothers' jar. But the golden flask would not hold the water. No matter how much was poured into it, it remained empty.

The emperor regarded the two young men sternly. "I believe you have tried to deceive me," he said. "You have brought me nothing but ordinary water."

The brothers began to tremble with such fear that the emperor knew he had discovered the truth. He ordered that the two young men be thrown into prison. Then once again he sent word throughout the land, imploring his people to redouble their efforts to find the magic lake. This time the emperor promised to reward whoever found the magic lake with whatever his heart desired.

When word of the brothers' disgrace reached the farmer and his wife, they were devastated. To lose both sons at once was a terrible blow. Harvesttime had come, and now there was no one to help with the work. They would surely starve to death.

When little Sumac saw her mother's tears and her father's grim, sad expression, she decided she herself would go and search for the magic lake.

"Hasn't the emperor promised to grant the heart's desire of whoever brings him the magic water? If I find the lake, then he will let my brothers go free."

At first her parents refused to let her go, but Sumac was such a headstrong little girl, and she argued and pleaded so incessantly that at last her parents, distracted by the grief of losing their two eldest children, agreed to let her go.

Sumac saddled up her favorite llama, and her mother gave her a woven bag full of roasted corn to carry with her on her journey. Too excited and full of hope to worry about the dangers that might lie before her, she cheerfully kissed her parents good-bye and followed the road leading out of the valley and into the wilderness.

On the first night, Sumac camped by the banks of a rocky stream, warmed by her llama. All went well, and the next day she continued bravely through the forest. But as night fell, she heard the cries of puma hunting in the bushes. She unsaddled her llama and sent it home, fearing for its safety. Then she stored her bag of corn in the hollow of a tall tree. Nestled in the highest branches of the tree, she fell asleep, far out of reach of the hungry cat.

As the sun rose, she was awakened by the gentle voices of a flock of sparrows resting on a nearby branch. They were eating the corn she'd hidden in the hollow of the tree.

"Poor little girl," one of the sparrows was saying. "She'll never be able to find the magic lake by herself."

"If only we could help her," another sparrow chirped.

"I think we *should* help her," the first sparrow said to her companions. "After all, she did share her corn with us."

Sumac stirred, and the sparrows twittered in surprise. "Oh, please, do you think you could help me?" she pleaded. "If I don't find the magic lake, my brothers will die in prison and my parents will die of broken hearts. Oh, please help me!"

"So you are awake, little girl," the first sparrow greeted her. "Yes, we shall help you."

Then each of the birds gave Sumac a wing feather.

"Hold the feathers together like a fan," one sparrow instructed her. "The fan is magic and will carry you wherever you wish to go. The feathers will also protect you from harm."

Sumac tied the feathers together using a ribbon from her hair. After thanking the sparrows with all her heart, she held the fan in front of her face and wished herself at the end of the world, beside the magic lake.

No sooner had she wished than a great wind plucked her out of the tree and whirled her around and around. Finally it set her gently down by the shore of a beautiful lake filled with crystal-clear waters of blue and green that lay as still as a mirror.

She ran to the lake's edge and cupped some of the water in her hands. It was as smooth as cream and as sweet as honey. Sumac was about to fill her jar with water for the prince when she had a terrible thought — she had left everything back in the forest. She had no jar with which to carry the water!

The little girl sat down on the sand and started to cry. "Why didn't I remember to bring a jar?" she sobbed out loud. "Oh, I wish I had something to carry the water back in."

Suddenly she heard a soft thud in the sand beside her. She looked and saw a golden flask — the same flask the emperor had found in the ashes.

Drying her eyes, Sumac hurried to fill the flask with water from the magic lake. But as she knelt at the water's edge, she heard a dreadful hissing sound behind her. "Get away from my lake," a horrible voice said, "or I'll wrap my hairy legs about your little neck!"

Sumac turned around. There stood a giant crab, as large as a pig and as black as pine pitch, staring at her with hostile, beady eyes.

Trembling with fright, she pulled the magic fan from her waistband and held it in front of her face. As soon as the crab looked at it, he fell down on the sand in a deep sleep.

Once more, Sumac started to fill the flask. But this time she was startled by a fierce voice bubbling up from the water.

"Get away from my lake or I'll eat you, little girl," gurgled a giant green alligator. His enormous jaws snapped at her, and his long tail beat the surface of the lake so that great waves rose up from its center.

Sumac waited until the alligator swam closer. When he was almost close enough to reach out and bite her, she held up the fan. The alligator blinked. He drew back and sank beneath the surface of the lake.

Next the girl heard a whistling in the air. She looked up and saw a flying serpent. His scales were as red as blood, and sparks flew from his eyes.

"Get away from my lake or I'll burn you to ashes," shrieked the serpent, spitting tongues of flame at her head. But again Sumac held up her fan, and when the serpent saw it, he floated lazily to the ground, closed his eyes, and began to snore.

Her heart racing, Sumac waited for yet another monster to appear. Moments passed, but the lake remained quiet and peaceful. When at last she was sure it was safe, she filled her flask with the precious water. Then quickly, before the sleeping monsters could wake up again, she held the fan to her face and wished herself at the emperor's palace.

Again the great wind came and whirled her around and around. It carried her high over the trees, over mountain and valley, river and lake, forest and field, then dropped her gently outside the gates to the emperor's palace. In one hand she held the fan of magic feathers and in the other the golden flask.

A palace guard noticed the small girl looking up at the gates, clutching something

tightly to her chest. "Off with you," he ordered briskly, pushing her away. "No loitering by the palace."

Sumac had not come all this way simply to be sent off at the last moment. She stuck out her chin and looked straight up into the guard's eyes. "I need to see the emperor," she said firmly.

The guard laughed. "What does a little girl like you want with the emperor?" he asked.

"I have water from the magic lake," Sumac replied, holding out the golden flask for him to see.

Astonished, the guard quickly led her into the emperor's chambers. The young prince lay motionless on a bed by the fire. His eyes were closed, and his skin had grown pale and waxy. He was near death. The old emperor sat beside him, his shoulders bowed with grief, while the prince's mother held his hands in her own, weeping quietly.

Without wasting words, Sumac went straight to the prince and poured a few drops of the magic water between his lips. Soon he opened his eyes. Then color began to come back to his cheeks. He reached out for more of the water, and Sumac handed him the flask. He drank all it held. Before long he was sitting up in bed, his eyes shining brightly.

"I never imagined I could feel this wonderful," the prince said, laughing with amazement.

Now the emperor and his queen wept with joy. They hugged Sumac and asked her again and again how she had found the magic lake. Sumac, who felt quite comfortable with the powerful emperor, sat on his lap and told him the whole story from beginning to end.

"Dearest child," said the old man when he had heard the story, "all the riches of my empire could not repay you for saving my son's life. But I have promised you your heart's desire. Tell me what you wish for, and it will be yours."

"I have three wishes," Sumac answered. "Is that too many?"

"No, I think you have earned three wishes," the emperor replied gravely.

"First I wish that my brothers could go free again. I know what they did was wrong, but they were only trying to help my parents."

"Guards, free them at once!" the emperor commanded.

"My second wish is that the magic fan be returned to the forest, so that the sparrows may have their feathers again," Sumac continued.

At these words, a gentle breeze blew in through the window. It lifted the feathers from her hand and whisked them off into the sky. Sumac watched them float away, waving good-bye. "Thank you, sparrows!" she called after them.

Finally she turned to the emperor and made her third wish. "Please, could you give my parents a larger farm, and great flocks of llamas, vicunas, and alpacas, so that we won't be poor any longer?"

"I am sure your parents never considered themselves poor with so wonderful a daughter," the emperor said, smiling and kissing her on both cheeks. "Nonetheless, your wish is granted."

Then the palace guards brought Sumac home to her family, where she found her brothers had been freed and her parents had received a deed granting them many acres of rich farmland. Her mother and father were overjoyed to see her, and they all lived well and happily the rest of their days.

GRANDMOTHER'S SKULL

A mother and father, two sons and one daughter lived by the great River Kobuk. Once they had been part of a large tribe with many families, but disease and war had killed all the others. Now they were only one family, and they knew no one else.

The sons were skillful hunters. There was plenty of game in the woods — caribou and bear, wolverine and fox. The family always had enough to eat. They never thought to travel down the river and visit the people by the sea.

The daughter's name was Neruvana. One day she went to fetch some water and saw a person who seemed to be growing from a tree trunk that was floating down the river. It was a young man paddling a kayak. She was astonished, for she'd never seen a kayak before, nor any person other than her mother and father and brothers. She ran home and told her family about it.

They all went down to the river to greet the stranger. Neruvana's father invited him to their house and made him welcome. That night they sat for hours talking to the young man. He told them he was from the people by the sea.

"What are you looking for?" the father asked him.

"I am looking for a wife," the young man answered with a smile.

The stranger stayed for many days. He went hunting with the brothers. He was a good hunter, and the family never grew tired of listening to his stories about the people who lived by the sea. One evening, after a month had passed, the father took the stranger aside.

"If you are really looking for a wife," he said, "you can marry my daughter. As you know, we are the last of our people, and I have no other hope of finding a husband for her."

The stranger agreed to this, and he and Neruvana were soon married. At first they were happy, but after a few weeks, Neruvana's new husband became restless.

"I'm taking my wife reindeer hunting," the young man told her family. "We'll travel upriver in my kayak, and we'll be back when we've filled the boat with meat."

They traveled far upriver and made camp in a place Neruvana had never seen before. Each day her husband went out hunting and left her by herself. Sometimes he would be gone for two or three days at a time. Once he was gone for more than a week. She had no idea where he could be and was terrified that something might have happened to him. But at last he came back and told her it was time to go home to her family.

They paddled down to the house, and the young woman called to her mother and father. But no one came to the river to greet them. She ran ashore to find out what had happened, and when she came to her house, she saw a terrible sight. All of her family — her mother and father and two brothers — had been murdered. Someone had stabbed them to death as they lay sleeping.

Screaming and weeping with grief and horror, Neruvana ran back to the shore to find her husband. But when she came to the bank of the river, she was shocked to see her husband paddling quickly away. She shouted to him, and he called back that he would land, yet he continued paddling downstream. She ran after him along the bank.

"My husband, come back! Please come back!" she pleaded, but the strange young man only paddled more rapidly away from her, and soon the river carried him out of sight.

Neruvana thought she was having an awful nightmare, but she could not wake up from this bad dream. She stumbled back up the river toward her old home, not knowing where to go or what to do.

After a time, she came to a place where there was high, soft grass. In exhaustion and despair, she fell to her knees and sobbed until she was empty of tears. Finally she could cry no more, and she fell asleep.

When she woke, she heard a soft voice calling her name. At first she thought she must be dreaming, but again and again she heard the same voice.

"Neruvana," the voice called, "Neruvana, dig me out!"

Neruvana looked around and discovered that she was lying by an old grave. The voice was coming from beneath the earth. "Neruvana, dear child, dig me out!"

Neruvana began to dig. She used a stick and her bare hands to scratch through the earth, until at last she dug a little skull out of the ground. She held the skull in her hands. Magically, it spoke to her.

"Neruvana," the skull said, "do you know who I am?"

Neruvana shook her head.

"I am the skull of your grandmother. Now that you have dug me out of the earth, you will not die, for I am here to protect you. First, dear child, you must make yourself a shelter, for night is coming."

Neruvana placed the skull tenderly on the ground and gathered branches to make herself a shelter for the night. When she finished, the sun had already set and she was shivering with cold.

"Little granddaughter," the skull said, "we are freezing. Fetch some dry brushwood and make a fire."

Neruvana did as the skull asked, and that night she slept warm and safe beside the fire.

The next day, the skull told her to make herself a house out of tree trunks and earth. She followed the skull's instructions carefully, and by the end of the day, she had built herself a small house that was sturdy enough to shelter her through the long winter.

"Now you have a house that will keep you warm and dry," the grandmother's skull told her. "But you must have food, or you will surely die. Tomorrow you will learn how to hunt."

Neruvana's grandmother told her how to make weapons for hunting and how to build traps for catching rabbits and beaver. She knew all the best places for setting traps and told her where to find the caribou.

Neruvana became as skilled a hunter as her brothers had been. She built a storehouse for meat and soon filled it. She scraped and dried the skins of wolverine and fox to make warm clothes and blankets.

The winter snows came and covered the ground. The trees bent low under the heavy weight of ice and snow, and the river froze. The grandmother's skull taught Neruvana how to catch fish by chopping a hole through the deep ice on the river.

During the long, quiet nights of winter, Neruvana's grandmother told her many stories. She told her about the days of her own childhood, when many people lived by the river. She taught her the secrets of the animals and all the things she would ever need to know to live in the woods by herself.

One day the skull asked her a question. "Dear child, do you know who killed your father and mother and brothers?"

Neruvana had grown wise from listening to her grandmother's stories night after night. "I believe it was my husband who killed them," she said. "But I still don't understand why or how."

"He is an evil man, my granddaughter, not fit for the responsibility of marriage or fatherhood. He easily grew tired of his marriage to you, and he thought that if he killed your family, he could return to his own people and they would never know of his marriage. While you were camping in the woods, he traveled by foot to your family's house and killed your mother and father and brothers while they were sleeping. Then he re-

turned to fetch you and his kayak. He took you to your parents' camp and left you there, thinking you would die of hunger.

"My own husband was like him. That is why I took pity on you and my spirit returned to earth to help you. In the spring your husband will come back, believing you dead, and try to take this beautiful country for himself and his people. My grandchild, you must not allow him to live on the land of your ancestors. In the springtime, when the river thaws and the hunting begins, he will lead some of his people to this place. They will come in their kayaks. When they come, we must be ready for them. Build a shelter by the river. Every day, we will watch and wait. When your husband comes, we will know how to welcome him."

The winter passed. The sun's warmth soon melted the snow, and the river ice burst with the current and the heat. The land came to life again and everything turned green as spring arrived in the forest.

One day the grandmother said, "Today is the day your husband will come, dear child. We must be ready."

Neruvana took her grandmother's skull down to the hiding place and waited. It wasn't long before she saw many boats coming around the bend in the river. The travelers were people she didn't know, and she let them pass. Then, at the end of the line of boats, she saw her husband.

The young woman burst from her hiding place and stood tall on the bank of the river. "Boats! Boats!" she cried in a strong voice.

Her husband looked up and saw her standing there. His mouth fell open in surprise. "My wife! You're alive!" he called, and started paddling toward her.

"Now is the time," the grandmother's skull whispered, and Neruvana hurled the skull into the river. Immediately the water began to bubble and boil, making whirlpools that seized her husband's boat, dragging it down to the bottom of the river. But the skull came rolling back to the bank as if nothing had happened and lay at Neruvana's feet.

"Neruvana," her grandmother told her, "your husband is dead now. He can never hurt you again. Take me back to our house and bury me where you found me. Now you are free to go where you will, for I've taught you all you need to know to survive in this world. If you like, follow these people who passed by in the boats. They are good people, and you can find a place with them. Or perhaps you would rather follow the paths of this forest to where they lead you. Wherever you go, dear child, remember your grandmother is always near you."

So Neruvana buried her grandmother's skull and continued on her way. Whether she settled with the people of the sea or traveled on to some farther country, no one can say for sure. But wherever she went, she carried her grandmother's wisdom with her.

THREE WHISKERS FROM A LION'S CHIN

aria and Pedro had loved each other for as long as they could remember. They grew up in the same village, and all through their childhood they played together, fishing in the river or riding into the jungle to look for wild fruit. Maria played the flute, and Pedro played the guitar, and together they made beautiful music for the whole village to dance to. This is how it always was with them, for they were born to be best of friends.

Time passed, and Maria grew into a beautiful young woman who was kind and hardworking, and Pedro grew into a handsome young man, strong and full of laughter. When it came time for the young people to marry, no one was surprised that Pedro and Maria decided to marry each other. Their parents gave them their blessings and helped them build a new house where, they hoped, their two fine children would raise many grandchildren.

But soon after the marriage, a war began, and soldiers came into the village looking for young men to join their army. Pedro was forced to leave with the soldiers, and for several years, Maria heard nothing from him. She didn't know if he was alive or dead. She cried many tears for her husband and spent many sleepless nights praying that by some miracle he would return to her safely.

At last, when five years had passed, Maria's prayers were answered. Pedro stumbled back into the village, thin as a skeleton, carrying nothing but the ragged clothes on his back, and gravely wounded, but still alive. Maria wept with joy to see him again. She took him home and carefully nursed him back to health, keeping watch over him day and night.

She cooked him all his favorite foods and fed him like a baby. She made new clothes for him and played her flute for him and told him little stories of life in the village to amuse him. Soon Pedro's wounds healed, and he became strong again. But something was still not right. Although Pedro's body healed, his spirit did not.

Instead of returning to work and tending his farm, he passed the days sitting in the house with the curtains drawn, drinking tequila and talking to himself. He never played his guitar anymore. When Maria encouraged him to go out and see his old friends or to walk with her through their garden, he raged that she should give him some peace. When she brought him food to eat, he threw it on the floor and smashed the dishes to pieces, screaming at her to leave him alone.

In desperation, Maria went to visit a *bruja* who lived by the edge of the forest. She explained her problem and begged the old woman to give her a charm that could bring her husband back to her. "For it's as if he has never truly come home from the war," she said. "His body is here with me, but his mind is still far away, seeing terrible sights and hearing terrible sounds."

"I can easily make you a charm," the old woman told Maria. "There is only one small difficulty. I am missing a special ingredient, and without it the charm cannot possibly work. You must bring me three whiskers plucked from the chin of a mountain lion. Then I will help you with your husband's problem."

Maria thanked the old woman with all her heart and ran joyfully back to her house. Not wanting to waste any time, she quickly gathered together her machete, her flute, and a new baby goat, which she tied in a sack and slung across her back. Then she set out to find the lion.

Maria followed the trail that led along the river. Deeper and deeper into the jungle she walked. It was dark and cool. The forest hummed with the cries of birds and the buzz of insects. The path became narrower and narrower, and Maria had to cut her way through the bush with her machete. Still she followed the path fearlessly, for she knew she must find the lion. Suddenly she heard a rustling sound. A snake slid out from among the trees and curled itself across the path, blocking her way. When Maria tried to step forward, the snake hissed at her, twisting its scaly head and flicking a venomous tongue in her direction. She raised her machete and chopped off the snake's head in one blow. Then she continued on her way.

Maria arrived at a bend in the river where the trees hung low over the water. There she heard a lion's roar. It was coming from somewhere above her head. She looked up and saw the little *pájaro león*, the lion bird that follows the lion and roars just as he does. She knew this must be the lion's watering hole. She tied the baby goat to one of the low-hanging branches and hid herself in the bushes.

Evening came, and the mosquitoes descended on her in droves, tormenting her with

their high-pitched whining and stinging bites. She gritted her teeth and tried not to mind them, keeping very still. Leaves from the *picapica* plant brushed at her bare arms and ankles, leaving terrible itching welts across her skin. She dug her nails into the palms of her hands and forced herself not to scratch. She waited for the lion.

The moon rose high in the night sky, turning the still waters of the river to a ribbon of silver, and at last the lion came out of the jungle to drink. Arriving at the riverbank, the lion raised his enormous head and gave a tremendous roar. When he saw the baby goat hanging from the low branch, he sprang on it and quickly devoured it. Then he drank deeply from the river. Content as a kitten with a belly full of milk, the lion threw himself down on the sandy bank to sleep.

Quietly and calmly, Maria crept from her hiding place with her flute in her hand. She crawled slowly toward the lion and knelt on the sand beside him. Then she began to play the songs of her childhood on her flute, softly and sweetly. The lion stretched and purred with pleasure. Still playing, Maria edged a little closer to him. She continued playing for a long time, until she was sure the great beast was sleeping soundly. Ever so gently, she began to stroke the lion's head, cradling it in her lap. When she judged that he was used to her hands and would not wake up, she reached over and plucked three whiskers from under his chin. The lion stirred and growled, but Maria kept stroking his head, and soon he was sleeping as peacefully as before.

Gently as a mother with a new baby, Maria slid the sleeping lion's head from her lap. Then she crawled back into the bushes and crept through the undergrowth to the forest path. Once she had reached the path, she ran as quickly as her legs could carry her and arrived at the village by dawn.

She burst into the *bruja*'s house without knocking, her clothes torn, her cheeks streaked with mud, her arms and legs red and swollen with mosquito bites and a burning rash from the *picapica* plant. The healer was sitting by the fire, waiting for her.

"I have them!" Maria cried excitedly, handing the *bruja* the three whiskers she'd plucked from the lion's chin. "How soon can I have my charm?"

The old woman took the three hairs and put them in her pocket. Then she looked at Maria silently for a few minutes. At last she spoke.

"Thank you, my dear," she said with a smile. "Now go back to Pedro and remember how you made your way through the jungle tonight. Remember the snake that crossed your path, the bushes and brambles that held you back, the mosquitoes that tormented you, the *picapica* plant that burned you. Remember how gently you rocked the fierce lion to sleep. Surely if you could manage to pull three whiskers from the chin of a live lion, you don't need the help of an old woman like me to bring your husband back to you."

DUFFY THE LADY

 t was cider-making time, and Squire Lovel went into town to find a housekeeper for his fine house on the hill. His old housekeeper had first gone blind in one eye, then deaf in one ear, then been crippled with arthritis, till finally she died, and now the place was a shambles.

The first thing that caught his attention when he rode into the village was Janey Chygwyn, beating her hired woman, Duffy, over the head with a frying pan.

"Hey, Janey," cried the squire from high on his shiny black horse, "what's the trouble with you and Duffy?"

"This lazy slattern spends all her time gossiping down at the corn mill and can't find half a minute during the day to spin yarn or knit stockings!" Janey shouted, taking another swipe at Duffy with the frying pan before she remembered her manners and curtsied to the squire.

"Don't believe her, your honor," Duffy exclaimed. "My knitting and spinning are the best in the county."

"Could you knit me new socks and sweaters and weave some cloth for woolen trousers?"

"I could, my lord," said Duffy, and Janey snorted loudly.

"Well, Duffy," said the squire, "come home with me, then, for I've need of a house-keeper. I haven't so much as one pair of socks without holes in them. Old Janey will be glad to be rid of you, and I'll be glad to have you."

So Duffy climbed up behind the squire on the horse and went home with him.

When Duffy saw the squire's manor, with dust everywhere and cobwebs on the candlesticks, dishes that hadn't been washed for over a month, and ashes overflowing in the fireplace, she knew she had her work cut out for her. Still, a job is a job, and better to work for Squire Lovel than complaining old Janey Chygwyn. She did a little dusting, built up a fire in the kitchen stove, and cooked the squire his first decent meal in many a month. But when she saw the room where the spinning was done, with wool piled high to the ceiling, she shut the door and went back to the kitchen to bake the squire an apple pie for his dessert. For the truth must be told: Duffy could neither knit nor spin.

The squire was happy to have his house back in order and was pleased with Duffy's cooking. But after a few days, he started wondering about the new socks and sweaters and woolen trousers Duffy had promised to make him.

"Well, I've had my hands full putting this house in order, my lord," Duffy told him. "But I'll get to it this very day."

"See you do, Duffy," the squire said sternly, and that afternoon Duffy went back to the spinning room to see what she could do.

She sat down at the spinning wheel and spun it around a few times to shake off the dust, but then she hadn't the slightest idea of what to do next. "Oh, curse this knitting and spinning!" she cried in frustration. "The devil may spin for the squire for all I care."

No sooner had she spoken when who should walk out of the corner but a spiffy little man dressed all in black, with a tail wrapped around his waist and horns on his head. Duffy recognized him right away for the devil he was, but not knowing what else to do, she greeted him politely and asked him what his business was.

"Well, Duffy, my dear, I heard you calling me."

"You did?" asked Duffy, astonished.

"Certainly I did. You'd like me to do all this spinning and knitting for you, wouldn't you? And I'm here to tell you I'd be happy to oblige."

Now, Duffy was nobody's fool, and she knew better than to accept an offer like that without reading the fine print in the contract. "If you do all that for me, what do you want me to do for you?" she asked him, narrowing her eyes suspiciously.

"Why, not a thing!" cried the gentleman, with a wounded expression on his face. "I'd be happy to help you out, and I don't want a penny in return.

"Of course," he added, speeding it up a little, "you'd have to agree to go away with me and be my lady after three years. Unless, that is, you could guess my name."

Duffy looked the devil straight in the eye. "Now let me be sure I understand. You'll do all the knitting and spinning for me, but after three years, I've got to go away with you?"

The devil nodded. "That's the deal," he said.

"But," Duffy continued, "if I guess your name before the three years is up, I don't have to go?"

"That's right," said the devil. "All you have to do is guess my name."

Duffy thought about it. If she accepted the devil's offer, she had three years to find out his name, and surely she could do that. But if she didn't take him up on it, the squire was bound to kick her out as soon as he found out she couldn't knit or spin.

"I accept your bargain," she declared. Duffy and the devil shook hands on it, and the deal was done.

After that, Duffy found that all she had to do was wish for something, and so it would be. The first thing she wished for was a pair of strong woolen socks, and when the squire came back from hunting that evening, she presented them to him. He was pleased as could be. Every day she wished for something new — a pair of socks or a warm sweater — and soon the squire had drawers full of socks and sweaters and jackets and fine woolen trousers. The squire boasted up and down the county that his hired woman spun the strongest, warmest wool in the country.

The months passed by, and Duffy kept the devil busy knitting and spinning. Meanwhile, she had plenty of time to spend down at the corn mill with the other women, telling jokes and stories or dancing on the green while the corn was being ground.

One evening Squire Lovel came home from hunting and found Malcolm the gardener waiting in the lane, while Duffy swung on the gate laughing. "What's he after?" the squire grumbled.

Duffy giggled. "Well, I expect he's courting me," she said, and the squire started to worry that maybe Duffy would get herself married and leave him all alone in that great house, with no one to fix him supper or knit stockings so warm that his feet never got cold even if he went out hunting all day and night in the worst of weather.

The next evening, he found Farmer Groundsel had come to call on Duffy, and he grew even more worried. He made up his mind to fix things so that Duffy was bound to stay with him forever. "Duffy," he said, "would you like to be a squire's lady?"

Duffy grinned from ear to ear. "I surely would, my lord," she answered him. So Duffy and the squire got married, and she became Duffy the lady and was happy as a cat with a big bowl of cream.

The three years the devil had promised her passed much more quickly than Duffy ever imagined, and try as she might, she couldn't discover his name. Finally there was only a week to go before her time was up.

In desperation, Duffy went down to the mill to talk to Old Bet, the miller's wife. Bet was known to be a witch, and if ever Duffy needed the help of a witch's magic, the time was now. She told Bet the story from beginning to end, and the old woman promised to help her.

"Bring me a jug of the strongest cider from the squire's cellar," she told Duffy. "Tonight's the full moon, and we're meeting down at Fugoe Hole. Your devil's bound to show up, and I'll get his name out of him for you. Whatever you do, don't go to sleep tonight until

73

the squire gets home from the hunt, no matter what the hour, and whatever he says, don't say a word back."

The moon rose red that night, and Duffy waited anxiously for the squire to come home. The church bells in the village chimed eleven times, then twelve times, but still the squire did not return, although after midnight his dogs straggled into the yard, panting and wet with sweat.

Finally, as the night sky began to lighten toward dawn, the squire came galloping into the courtyard. He leapt from his horse and kissed his Duffy lady soundly. "Why, m'dear, you'll never guess what I saw tonight," he cried, laughing loudly. But Duffy just bit her tongue and said not a word.

"I'd been hunting all day, without any luck," the squire continued, "and I was ready to head home when we startled a hare. The dogs chased her across the down, all the way to Fugoe Hole, and there we lost her. I was rounding the hill, and what do you imagine I saw, Duffy? Why, it was the witch's dance. They'd lit a great fire, and they were singing and playing the tambourine. Bless my soul, I couldn't tear myself away from the sight. So I hid behind some bushes, and then I saw a spiffy little man dressed all in black. He was dancing around the fire, and every time he danced to the west he took a swig from the jug of cider he held in his hand and jumped up and down and laughed like a madman. If only you could have seen it, Duffy. And can you imagine what he was singing?"

Now Duffy was ready to die with impatience, for of course she hadn't a clue what the old devil was singing, and of course that was what she needed to know. But she kept her peace and just shook her head and waited for the squire to tell her in his own time.

"He was singing about you, Duffy!" the squire cried, roaring with laughter. "He was dancing and singing:

> 'Duffy, my lady, you'll never know — what?
> That my name is Terrytop, Terrytop, Terry — top!'

I swear, Duffy, if only you could have seen it!"

Still laughing, the squire went off to bed, and Duffy went with him. For the first time in many weeks, she slept soundly.

The next day, the three years were up. Duffy had wished for an abundance of knitted things and was in the bedroom, trying to cram some more stockings into a big chest, when the spiffy little man in black appeared before her.

"Well, Duffy, my dear," he said, "I've kept my promise and served you faithfully for three years, so now I hope you're ready to go away with me, as we agreed."

"I'm afraid your country is rather warm," Duffy said with a smile. "It might ruin my fair complexion."

"It's not as hot as some people say," the devil replied. "Come, now. Can you guess my name?"

"Let me see," Duffy sighed, sounding uncertain. "Could it be Lucifer?"

"Lucifer?" the little man cried, stamping his feet. "I wouldn't be caught dead with that scoundrel. Certainly not!"

"Hmmm," murmured Duffy, scratching her head. "Is it Beelzebub?"

The devil snorted. "Beelzebub! He might be a distant cousin, but he's nothing but a common devil, you know."

"Well, sir," said Duffy with a little curtsy, "I hope you're honest enough to admit your real name is Terrytop."

The devil stood up tall (as tall as a little man like him could rise) and bowed deeply. "A gentleman never denies his name. Still, I never expected to be beaten by a lazy slattern like you, Duffy."

And with those words, he disappeared. In the very same moment, all the knitted things he'd made for Duffy over the last three years turned to dust and blew away.

The squire came home an hour later, chilled to the bone and wearing nothing but his shirt and shoes. It seems that while he was out hunting on the moors, his socks and trousers and jacket had suddenly fallen from his back.

"It's witchcraft," Duffy warned. "This morning when I was tidying up I heard a bang, like thunder, and a flash of light, and suddenly every woolen thing in this house disappeared. The witches have cursed you for spying on their dance. Now every time I try to spin, the yarn breaks in my hands. From now on, we'd best have our woolen things made in the village. You wouldn't want to have your clothes disappearing on you while you're out hunting every day — you'd be a laughingstock, and catch your death of cold on top of it."

The squire saw the wisdom in her words, and from that day on he never asked Duffy to do a stitch of knitting or spinning.

SUN-GIRL AND DRAGON-PRINCE

nce there was a poor peasant's daughter whose name was Arevhat, or Sun-Girl, for her smile would brighten even the darkest of days.

When Arevhat was eight years old, her mother died. Her father soon married another woman, who was jealous of Arevhat and determined to make her miserable. Every day she sent her stepdaughter out to the fields to tend the sheep. She packed Arevhat's bag with just a stale crust of bread to eat — and a pound of wool to card before she could come home at night.

Arevhat worked every day from morning late into the night, carding wool and tending the sheep. She was constantly hungry and lonely and weary. Still she grew brighter and more beautiful with each passing year, for her heart was as warm and loving as the sun itself.

One day, when Arevhat sat carding wool on the edge of a rocky cliff, she dropped her carding comb onto the ledge below her. She climbed down to fetch it and saw a small cave in the side of the cliff. At the mouth of the cave was an old woman, holding Arevhat's comb.

"Good day, Granny," Arevhat said. "I dropped my carding comb. May I have it back, please?"

"In a minute, child," the old woman replied. "Come here. I want to talk to you."

Arevhat went into the cave and saw that it was like a little house. The old woman handed her a broom and told her to sweep the floor.

"Tell me, child — whose house is cleaner, yours or mine?" the old woman asked.

The old woman's cave was filthy, but Arevhat didn't want to say that. "Your house is cleaner, Granny," she replied kindly, and the old woman looked happy.

When Arevhat had finished sweeping, the old woman asked her to comb her hair. As she lay her head on Arevhat's lap, Arevhat could see that her hair was full of lice and was as greasy and snarled as a bundle of wool. Nonetheless, she began gently combing out the tangles.

"Tell me, child — whose hair is cleaner, mine or your mother's?" the old woman asked.

"Your hair is cleaner," Arevhat answered, and the old woman smiled in satisfaction.

"I'm getting sleepy," said the crone. "Let me sleep with my head in your lap. While I sleep, a stream of water will begin flowing through this house. First the water will be black. Then it will become red. When the water becomes yellow, wake me up and tell me about it."

The old woman fell asleep. Just as she had said, a stream of water suddenly came flowing through the cave. It flowed with black water. Then the water turned red. When the water became yellow, Arevhat shook the old woman awake. "Granny, wake up! Here is the yellow water!"

The old woman jumped up and seized Arevhat by the legs. She was as strong as a giant, even though she was so old. She pushed the young girl's head all the way under the water. When Arevhat stood up, her hair had turned the color of gold, as bright and shining as the sun. Then the old woman sent her away. "Go, child. And my blessings go with you," she said.

Arevhat thought that if she went home with golden hair, her stepmother would be furious with her and probably tear every hair from her head. In a daze, she wandered through the fields, not knowing where to go or what to do. Soon she came to a road she had never seen before. She decided to follow the road and see where it would lead her.

Before she had walked very far, she heard the pounding of horses' hooves, and in a few moments, the horses and their riders had caught up to her. It was a band of the king's soldiers, out searching the countryside for young girls to feed to the king's son. Years before, the queen of that country had given birth to a terrible monster — half human, half dragon — and all he would eat were young maidens.

The soldiers had noticed Arevhat from down the road, because of her golden hair. They whisked her up and carried her back to the palace to feed to the hungry dragon-prince. They dropped her into the pit where the prince was kept — so roughly that she fell and broke her tooth on the floor.

The hideous monster roared when he saw the girl and rose up to devour her. But Sun-Girl wasn't afraid. She smiled at him and said, "Good evening, king's son!"

When Dragon-Prince saw her smile, his heart knew warmth for the first time. He began to weep. As the tears ran down his scales, they melted away. Soon all the dragon part of him had disappeared. He became a young man like any other, except that he was very handsome. He took Sun-Girl in his arms and kissed her. Then he gave her a jewel to replace her broken tooth, a diamond that shone as brightly as her smile and reflected his own face.

The king's soldiers came back and peered down into the den to see if Dragon-Prince had finished eating. Instead they saw a handsome young man embracing the maiden with golden hair, and they ran to tell the king and queen. The king and queen hurried to the dragon's den. When they realized that their only son had been transformed into an ordinary young man, they wept with joy.

The prince then took Arevhat's hand. "This is the girl who changed me from a dragon to a man," he said. "And I want to marry her." The king and queen were delighted, for Arevhat seemed as sweet and beautiful as an angel. The palace was filled with laughter and rejoicing.

The wedding banquet lasted for seven days and seven nights. The entire kingdom celebrated the marriage of the young prince to the beautiful Sun-Girl. Arevhat invited her father and stepmother to the wedding, and they acted as though they were very happy for her. But in truth, Arevhat's stepmother was enraged with jealousy. She pretended to treat Arevhat like a beloved daughter, but she hated her so much, she wanted to kill her.

One day after the wedding, Arevhat's stepmother asked her to come down to the river so that the two women could do their washing together. Dragon-Prince didn't want her to go — he didn't like the way the stepmother looked at his wife, with such cold, bitter eyes. But Arevhat only laughed. She wanted to believe that her stepmother really cared for her, so she took her washing to the river just as they had arranged.

While Arevhat was leaning over the riverbank scrubbing her clothes, the stepmother came quietly behind her. She pushed her as hard as she could, and Sun-Girl fell into the deep part of the river. The current was so strong, she couldn't swim to shore, and she was swept downstream. The stepmother then went back to the palace and told everyone that Arevhat had fallen into the river by accident and drowned.

She hadn't drowned, however, for luckily she saw a log floating down the river. She grabbed the log and hung on to it for her life. For three days and three nights, she clung to the log while the river carried her farther and farther away from her kingdom. Finally the current grew weaker, and with the bit of strength that remained to her, Arevhat managed to swim to shore.

The land she had come to was a vast and lonely desert. The sun burned more fiercely than she had ever felt before. For many days she wandered without ever seeing another human soul. She lived on grasses and insects that she dug from the rocky earth. By day, the sun scorched her, and at night a cold wind blew across the barren plain and chilled her to the bone. Still she wandered on, putting one foot in front of the other, to see where her life would lead her.

One day she came to a little entryway made out of reeds and tree branches, leading into a cave. Peering through the door, she saw a man sleeping inside. She sat down by the door and waited.

When the sun went down, the man woke up. At first he was frightened, for he thought Arevhat was a ghost. After he realized she was a real girl, he asked her why she had come to this terrible place. Arevhat told him the story of everything that had happened to her. Then he told her his story.

"I am the son of a rich man," he began. "As a boy I had nothing to do all day but go hunting and enjoy life. Once, for three days, I had a streak of bad luck and found nothing to shoot. I became so angry that I wanted to shoot the sun. I didn't care if I plunged the whole world into darkness. I raised my bow, aiming at the sun, when suddenly a tongue of flame whirled me around and flung me to this desolate land, where I have to live in darkness. A voice cursed me and said I should never see the sun again, and that if I do, I shall die. So I sleep in this cave by day and go out only after dark."

Sun-Girl stayed with this man in his cave. He was a good man, but always sad. By day, he slept as deeply as the dead. At night he woke up and went hunting to provide them with food. Sun-Girl spent most of the time by herself. She didn't mind — she was used to a lonely life. Each day she walked for hours in the desert and sang songs about her sad life as a young girl, about how her hair had turned golden, and how she had been pushed into the river by her stepmother. She sang for the rocks and the trees and the sparse desert grass, and sang for the sun itself.

After three years, Arevhat and the hunter had a baby, a little boy. Sun-Girl realized that this was no life for her child, with a father who spent all the day sleeping like a dead man and never saw the light of the sun. Every day she walked through the desert with her baby strapped to her back, wondering what to do. Then one night she dreamed of her real mother, who had died when she was eight years old. In the dream her mother said, "Go west in iron shoes. You will find a cure for this man and freedom for yourself."

Sun-Girl put on iron shoes, put her baby on her back, and walked west to the end of the earth and back again. When her iron shoes had worn apart, she came at last to a lofty palace of dazzling blue marble. She entered through the gate and passed through one court after another, under twelve golden arches so bright it hurt her eyes to look at them. The courts shimmered with blue pools, and fountains splashed in the deep silence of the castle. In the center she found a golden pavilion surrounded by stars. There she saw a queenly woman, taller than the tallest pine tree, lying on a bed of pearls. Arevhat was

frightened and turned to run from this place, but the great queen held out her arms to her and drew her up onto the pavilion.

"Tell me what's troubling you, my child," the woman said in a voice as soft and large and comforting as the wind blowing through the trees. "You have walked until your iron shoes were worn from your feet, and now you have earned the right to tell me your sorrows."

Then Sun-Girl held up her baby for the queen to see. "This boy's father has been cursed by the sun, and now can never know the light of day nor free himself from the terrible sadness of his dark life. How can he be a good father to my child?" And she told the queen her story.

"I am a mother, too," the queen replied when Arevhat was finished. "I am the mother of the sun, and I understand how you feel. But this baby's foolish father wanted to shoot my only child with a bow and arrow. That is why he is condemned to live in darkness, deprived of the sun's light."

"Save him, please, for my little boy's sake!" Arevhat cried.

The great queen took pity on her. "Many an unworthy man has enjoyed the blessings of the sun because of a mother's loving heart. Hide behind these stars. My son is coming home now, and I don't want you and your baby to burn to death when he arrives. He will bathe in this pool and become a baby again, for the sun is forever young, forever newly born. Then I will nurse him at my breast. While he drinks his mother's milk, take a bottle of water from the pool and go home. Sprinkle the water on your baby's father, and the curse will be lifted."

Arevhat hid behind the sleeping stars. Soon the sun arrived in a blaze of fire and dove straight into the marble pool before the golden pavilion. The stars shook themselves from their dreaming and greeted him. When he had finished bathing, the sun's mother lifted him out of the pool and carried him to her bed. While the sun-baby drank his mother's milk, Arevhat filled a bottle with water from the marble pool and ran out of the castle-of-the-sun.

She put her baby on her back and walked east to the end of the world and back again, until at last she arrived home. The lonely hunter lay sleeping in his cave. Arevhat sprinkled him with the magic water, and immediately he woke up and ran outside. For the first time in all the years of his exile, he saw the light of day. He laughed, a big long laugh that echoed out across the desert and changed that place, so that the barren wasteland became a lush and fertile valley.

Soon people from all over the world heard of the hunter's cure and the miraculous change that had come to the desert. Many visitors came to see the changes for themselves and to meet the woman who had been to the castle-of-the-sun. Among them was Dragon-Prince, who was still mourning for his lost Sun-Girl.

When Dragon-Prince arrived at the house, he recognized Sun-Girl right away, because of her diamond tooth and golden hair. Arevhat asked him to stay the night. She promised she would show him the green valley that had once been a desert.

The next day Arevhat took her baby and went riding with the hunter and Dragon-Prince. It was a hot day, and soon she became thirsty. "I'm thirsty," she called, and the hunter rushed to her right side and handed her a flask of water. At the same time, Dragon-Prince came to her left side. He, too, handed her a flask of water.

Arevhat stood between the two men, holding her baby.

"Take him — you are his father," she said to the hunter, handing him the baby. "I am going with Dragon-Prince. He is my husband."

Then Sun-Girl drank from the flask of water that Dragon-Prince gave her, and she rode away with him.

STAVER AND VASSILISSA

rand Duke Vladimir sat banqueting in the hall of his castle, surrounded by princes and warlords and all the heroes of his realm. The feasting continued for many hours, with plenty to eat and drink, and music to lighten the saddest heart.

After the heroes had eaten and drunk their fill, they began to boast, and no one boasted louder than the grand duke himself. Nowhere, he insisted, was there more gold, nowhere more silver, nowhere greater heaps of pearls than here in his fine palace. And where could one find a woman more beautiful than his own wife, the lovely Apraksiya?

This was too much for young Prince Staver. "Listen to him boasting," he murmured to his neighbor. "He thinks this stone box of his should be called a castle. My own castle is so large, it's better to ride through it on horseback than to walk. The floors are paved with silver, and the walls are built from bricks of gold. I have so many chests of pearls and diamonds and rubies, they could fill a room as big as this hall. But my greatest treasure of all is my wife, Vassilissa. Her hair is like that of a fox, her eyes as sharp as falcon's eyes. Not only is she a superb housekeeper, she's also stronger than any man in this hall."

While Staver was speaking, the hall grew quiet, and he looked up to see the grand duke's eyes upon him. His face was red with anger, and he bellowed like a wild boar, "So, Staver Godinovitch, you think you can insult me and humiliate me here in my own hall? Enough of your empty talk, you blithering idiot. Throw him in the dungeon! Then ride to his castle, seal it up with all his treasure chests within, and bring me the beautiful Vassilissa. Bring her to me, Grand Duke Vladimir!"

Staver was seized and thrown into the dungeon. Then ten of Vladimir's warlords rode off to seal up his castle and bring back Vassilissa.

But Staver's friend Mikhail Kolosov rode ahead of the others to warn Vassilissa of the grand duke's order.

Vassilissa tucked her long red hair under her helmet and dressed herself as a man. She took a stout sword from Staver's armory and sharpened her quiverful of arrows. Then she mounted her black stallion and, with twelve of her men, set out for the grand duke's castle.

Halfway there, she met the warlords who had been ordered to take her prisoner. They didn't recognize her and asked her where she was going.

"I've come from the Khan of the Golden Hordes," Vassilissa answered. "My men and I are here to remind Grand Duke Vladimir that he owes the khan tribute for the last twelve years. We have orders to take many chests of gold back to the khan. And where are you riding?"

"We're going to Staver's castle, to seal it up and carry his wife, Vassilissa, to the grand duke," said one of the warlords.

"We have just passed Staver's castle. Vassilissa is not there. She has ridden away," she told them.

So the band of warlords galloped back to the grand duke's castle and reported that Vassilissa was missing and that the ambassador from the Khan of the Golden Hordes was on his way to exact tribute. When Vassilissa arrived at the castle, everyone assumed she was the ambassador and treated her with great courtesy.

But Vladimir's wife, Apraksiya, was watching the new arrival carefully. "That's not the ambassador from the khan," she whispered to her husband. "Can't you tell that it's a woman? I think that's Staver's wife, Vassilissa. Look at how he walks!"

The duke observed the young ambassador carefully. Perhaps his wife was right. He decided to hold a wrestling contest to test the ambassador's strength. If this was a woman, she would surely lose.

"In this country, it is our custom that all visitors be given the opportunity to test their strength against my warlords," Vladimir told the ambassador. "If it pleases your excellency, we shall now hold a wrestling contest." Seven of his warlords immediately rose from the banqueting tables to challenge the disguised Vassilissa.

The first man stepped forth. Vassilissa threw him so hard that he had to be carried from the hall. The second had seven of his ribs broken by a single blow of her fist. The third had three of his vertebrae dislocated and had to crawl from the hall on his hands and knees. The rest of the challengers fled, not wishing to be humiliated before all their comrades.

Vladimir trembled with frustration and spat on the floor. "Your hair may be long," he

muttered to his wife, "but you haven't a brain in your head. Why did you tell me he was a woman? My court has never seen a hero with such strength!"

Apraksiya raised her eyebrows. "Look at that skin," she urged her husband. "Is that the skin of a man? And why does she always wear a helmet? Could she be hiding her long hair beneath it?"

Vladimir glared at his wife angrily. He blamed her for making him look like a fool. But he couldn't help wondering if she might be right, and he decided to put the khan's envoy to another test.

"I see you are very strong," he congratulated Vassilissa, slapping her heartily on the back. "Now perhaps you would like to prove your skill at archery."

With these words, he led his court to an open meadow behind the castle. All of Vladimir's men shot their arrows into an old oak that stood at the far end of the field. Each time it was hit, the oak tree swayed as if it were caught in a gust of wind. But when Vassilissa shot her arrow, the bowstring sang and the mighty oak shattered into a thousand pieces.

The men were dumbfounded.

Vladimir spat for the second time. "Look at that oak tree," he hissed at Apraksiya. "We've never seen such an archer before, and you believe he's a woman. I shall challenge him myself and see if he's also supreme at chess."

Vladimir and Vassilissa now sat down at the grand duke's chess table and played chess with chessmen carved from the finest marble. Vassilissa won the first game, and also the second, and the third. She laughed, for the duke had played for high stakes. Then she pushed the chessboard aside.

"Enough of this foolishness," she declared. "I didn't come here to feast with you or to waste my time playing games. What about the tribute you owe the great khan? You haven't paid for twelve whole years. I demand two chests of gold for every year. Produce them here and now! The Khan of the Golden Hordes refuses to wait any longer."

Then Vladimir began to whine. "Times are hard, you know. The harvest was poor this year and last. Merchants are doing little business, trade is slow, and we haven't collected much in taxes. How can I pay? Couldn't the great khan wait another year?"

Vassilissa tapped her fingers impatiently on the chess table. "He's already waited twelve years. I can't go back empty-handed. If you don't have gold, you must send something else."

"Perhaps he'd like my wife, Apraksiya," the grand duke suggested jokingly.

"What use would she be to the Khan of the Golden Hordes? He has many beautiful women. Have you someone who plays the lute?"

Suddenly Vladimir remembered that Staver was an excellent lute player. "Indeed I do," he replied promptly, "the finest lute player in the land. His name is Staver, one of my favorite princes. You are welcome to take him as a present to the great khan."

So Vladimir had Staver brought out of the dungeon, and Staver rode back to his castle with Vassilissa, where they lived happily ever after. As for the grand duke, he was pleased as could be that he'd managed to avoid paying tribute to the Khan of the Golden Hordes for yet another year.

TOKOYO

ong, long ago there lived a powerful emperor who had fallen sick with a mysterious illness. His bones ached, it was difficult for him to breathe, and he was always in great pain. His illness made him short-tempered and irritable, so that he easily became offended by any slight to his dignity, real or imagined. One day, for no particular reason, he grew furious with the noble samurai Oribe Shima and ordered the good man banished. Oribe Shima was sent to the Oki Islands, a wild and desolate place far from the court of the emperor, to live out the rest of his days in poverty and isolation.

Oribe Shima had only one child, a brave and spirited young woman named Tokoyo. From the time she was a tiny girl, Tokoyo had been in love with the sea, and she spent all her time with the women who dive for oysters deep down at the bottom of the ocean. By the time Tokoyo became a grown woman, she was the best of all the oyster divers, fearless and strong. Nobody could dive deeper or swim farther than she, and everyone admired her courage and endurance.

When Tokoyo learned of her father's banishment, she was heartbroken, and furious with the unjust emperor. She decided to find her father and to share his lonely exile with him. She sold all their property and walked to the small fishing village of Akasaki. There she tried to persuade the fishermen to take her to the Oki Islands, but not one wanted to help her. It was too long and dangerous a voyage. Besides, it was forbidden to visit those who had been banished, and the fishermen feared they would be punished if they helped her.

Finally Tokoyo spent the rest of her money on a small sailing boat. On a clear, moonless night, she slipped down to the harbor and set sail for the Oki Islands all by herself. It was a reckless thing to do, but good fortune smiled on her and sent her a strong breeze. The sea remained calm, and the following evening she arrived at a rocky cliff off one of the islands, exhausted and chilled to the bone. Since she could find nowhere to dock her boat, she tied a bundle of food and clothes to her head, tucked her oyster dagger into her belt, and swam to shore.

After resting all night in a small sheltered place between two rocks, she climbed the cliff to the road above. There she met a fisherman and immediately asked him if he had word of her father, Oribe Shima. No, the fisherman had never heard of this man. Tokoyo told the fisherman her story, and he warned her never to mention her father's name again, for if the emperor knew she was looking for him, he might easily have her father killed.

Tokoyo wandered from island to island, hoping to hear word of her father but afraid to ask about him. She managed to stay alive by begging food from some of the kind people she met along the way. Months passed, but she heard no mention of her father's name, and she began to fear he was no longer alive.

One night she came to a small shrine that had been built on a rocky ledge. She decided to pass the night there and curled up in the shadow of the shrine, her bundle tucked beneath her head. In a little while she was awakened by the sound of a girl sobbing and a curious clapping of hands. She opened her eyes, and in the bright moonlight she saw a young girl kneeling before a priest, who clapped his hands over her and chanted strange prayers.

Tokoyo was horrified to see the priest seize the frightened girl and drag her to the edge of the cliff. The girl screamed in terror. Just as he was about to push her into the angry sea below, Tokoyo raced from the shadows of the shrine and pulled the girl to safety.

"What are you doing?" she cried, pushing the priest away.

The priest looked at her sadly. "I can see you are a stranger to this place," he said quietly, "and not familiar with our customs. This island has been cursed by an evil god, Yofune-Nushi. He lives at the bottom of the sea and each year demands that we sacrifice a young girl to his kingdom. If we don't send what he demands, he becomes angry and causes great storms at sea, so that the boats of our fishing people are broken and many of the fishermen drown."

Tokoyo listened seriously to everything the priest said. Then she spoke.

"Holy monk, my name is Tokoyo, and I am the daughter of Oribe Shima, a noble samurai who was banished to these islands by the emperor. Months ago I came here looking for my father, but though I have searched and searched for him, I cannot find him, and now I believe I will never see him again. My life is no longer precious to me. Death would be a sweet release. But life is precious to this young girl. Allow her to go free, and I will take her place."

While the old priest looked on, Tokoyo untied the girl's hands and motioned for her to leave. Then she wrapped a white cloth around her head and knelt at the shrine to pray for courage. In her heart, she was determined to kill the evil god Yofune-Nushi. She took her oyster dagger from her bundle of clothes, placed it between her teeth, and dove into the water.

Down, down, down she plunged, into the icy water. A path of moonlight led her to the bottom of the sea, and Tokoyo allowed the current to pull her deeper and deeper. Finally she found herself at the mouth of an enormous cave with walls of mother-of-pearl, encrusted with jewels and seashells and glowing with an unearthly light. But the cave was empty except for a wooden statue. Swiftly she swam to the statue and saw it was a wooden likeness of the emperor himself, beautifully made, but tied tightly with ropes of black seaweed, which seemed to be strangling it.

At the sight of the emperor who had caused her so much grief, Tokoyo's heart filled with bitterness. She raised her dagger to strike angrily at the statue, but then she thought, What good would it do? Better to do good than evil. Quickly she undid her sash and tied the statue to her back. Then she began swimming upward.

As she left the cave, a horrible face rose up in front of her. It was covered with scales and had hundreds of tiny legs growing from its long, snakelike body. She knew it was Yofune-Nushi. A poisonous cloud of red issued from its black mouth and swirled about her, blinding her. But Tokoyo raised her dagger and struck deeply into the monster's rolling, lidless eyes, and then again at its heart. Squirming and wriggling with pain, the sea-god slumped to the ocean's floor and died. With her last ounce of strength, Tokoyo cut off the sea-god's head and began swimming upward with one hand. The water pressed in around her, and she began to see flashing lights behind her eyes. I am dying, she thought, but still she kept swimming. The path of moonlight guided her up and up, until somehow, gasping, she reached the surface, still clutching the horrible head of the dead sea-god.

The priest, lingering on the shore, was amazed to see Tokoyo emerge from the waves. He climbed down the cliff to the beach and carried her out of the water, then called for the islanders to come and help. When they saw the head of Yofune-Nushi, they knew they were at last free of the terrible curse. They buried the head deep in the sand and tenderly carried Tokoyo into the village, along with the statue of the emperor.

Word of the courageous diver who had killed the sea-god and rescued the emperor's statue soon reached the court of the emperor himself. Miraculously the emperor quickly recovered from the illness that had tormented him for so many years. He realized that he, too, had been cursed by the evil god. When he discovered that the person who had freed him from the sea creature's curse was the daughter of Oribe Shima, he immediately decreed the end of the samurai's banishment.

Tokoyo's father had been living in a lonely cottage far from any of the villages. Since he

was forbidden to speak to the islanders, none had known of his presence. The emperor's messengers came to tell him that his daughter was now a heroine and that he was free to return to his home.

At first he could not believe that his months of exile were truly over. But Tokoyo herself finally found her way to the cottage, and father and daughter were joyfully reunited. They returned to the court of the emperor, where they were received with great honor, and they lived the rest of their days in peace and prosperity.

THE LORD'S DAUGHTER AND THE BLACKSMITH'S SON

n old lord had a young daughter, and she was the most spoiled girl in all the world. Her father indulged her and her mother petted her till it was a wonder she could be tolerated. What saved her from being a horror was that she was so sunny and sweet by nature, with such a merry way about her, that she won all hearts. The only thing wrong with her was that once she set her mind on something, she wouldn't give up till she'd got what she wanted.

It wasn't much of a problem when she was a little girl, but as she was getting to be a young lady, that's when the trouble began. Her father decided it was time to find a husband for her, so he and her mother began looking around for a suitable match. It didn't take long for the girl to find out what they had in mind. So she began to do a bit of looking around on her own. Then one day as she was looking out her bedroom window, she saw a boy she might fancy in the courtyard below.

She called to her maid, "Come quick to the window! Who is the lad down below?"

The maid came and looked. "Oh, it's only the son of the blacksmith," she said. "No doubt the lord sent for him to shoe the new mare."

"Why have I never seen him before?" asked the girl.

"The blacksmith's shop is not a place for a young lady. Come away from the window now! Your mother would be in a fine state if she saw you acting so bold."

And no doubt she was right, for the girl was hanging over the windowsill in a most unladylike way.

She came away from the window, but she made up her mind to go down to the village for another look at the blacksmith's son. She liked the way he walked and the way his yellow hair swept back from his brow, and she had a good idea she'd like a lot of other things about him if she could get a better look at him.

She knew her mother would never let her go if she asked, so she just went without asking. To make sure nobody would know her, she borrowed the dairymaid's best dress. She didn't ask to borrow it, either; she just took it when nobody was around to see.

The blacksmith's shop was a dark place, but not so dark that she couldn't see the blacksmith's son shoeing the lord's horse. His coat was off and he had a great smudge of soot on his cheek, but she liked him even better than before.

"Good day," she said.

"Good day," he said, looking up in surprise. And he gave her a smile that turned her heart upside down.

So she gave him one as good in return. "I'm from the castle," she said. "I just stopped in to see how you were coming with the new mare."

"I've two shoes on and two to go," he said. "Wait here a bit and I'll give you a ride back to the castle as soon as I'm done."

"Oh, no!" said the lord's daughter. "I just stopped by. I can't be late coming home."

He begged her to stay, but she would not. He wasn't pleased to see her go, for he liked her terribly and wanted to know her better.

When he took the mare back, he tried to find out which of the maids from the castle had been in the village that day. But no one could tell him, for there were plenty of maids, and who knew which one might be coming or going? But whoever she was and wherever she was, she'd taken his heart along with her.

The lord's daughter came home and put the dairymaid's dress back where she'd found it. After she'd made herself tidy, she went to find her father and said, "You can just stop looking for a husband for me, because I've found the one I want myself. I'm going to marry the blacksmith's son."

At first the lord thought she was joking, but then he saw she was not. He flew into a terrible rage, but no matter what he said, it was of no use. His daughter had made up her mind, and he couldn't change it.

Well, the lord could only sputter and swear, and his lady could only sit and cry. They sent the girl to bed without her supper, but the cook smuggled it up to her on a tray, so that was no punishment at all.

The next morning the lord told her that she and her mother were going off to the city in a week's time. There she'd stay until she was safely married to her second cousin twice-removed. The lord had finally picked him to be her husband, and there were to be no questions about it.

"I'll go if I must," said the girl. "But you can tell my cousin I won't be marrying him. I've made up my mind to marry the blacksmith's son."

The blacksmith's son soon had his own troubles.

When the lord and his family came out of church that Sunday morning, they passed by the blacksmith and his son at the gate.

"Who's the lass with the lord and his lady?" he asked his father.

The blacksmith turned and looked. "You ninny!" he said in disgust. "Can't you see that's no lass you're looking at? That's a young lady. That's the lord's own daughter."

The blacksmith's son had been building cloud-castles about the girl he thought was one of the maids in the castle, and now they all tumbled down. His heart was broken.

The day before the girl and her mother were to leave for the city, the girl rose from her bed at the break of dawn and tiptoed downstairs. Since this was her last day at home, she wanted to have a little time to herself.

The cook was in the kitchen as she passed by, picking something up off the floor.

"What have you there?" asked the girl.

"It's a baby's shoe," said the cook. "One of the lord's dogs brought it in and dropped it on the floor. It's a pretty little shoe, isn't it?"

"Give it to me," said the girl. "I'll find the baby who owns it." She took the shoe and put it in her pocket.

Around the stables and through the kitchen garden she went, to the lane that led to the gardener's house. Halfway there she saw a little man sitting by the side of the lane with his head in his hands. He was crying as if his heart would break. He was no bigger than a child, and indeed, he looked like a child, sitting there and crying so hard, and she sat down and put her arms around him to comfort him. "Don't be sad," she said. "Tell me your trouble, and if I can I'll fix it."

"It's my shoe!" wailed the tiny little man. "I took it off to take a stone out of it, and a great dog came and snatched it out of my hand and ran off with it. I can't walk over the briars and brambles and cruel sharp stones without my shoe, and I'll never get home today."

"Well, now!" said the girl with a laugh. "I think I can fix your troubles easier than my own. Is this the shoe you're looking for?" And she put her hand in her pocket and took out the shoe she'd taken from the cook.

"Yes, yes, that's it!" cried the little man. "It's my pretty little shoe!" He grabbed it from her hand and put it on and, springing into the road, he danced for joy. But in a minute he was back, sitting on the bank beside her.

"Fair is fair," he said. "What are your troubles? Maybe I can mend yours as you did mine."

"Mine are past mending," sighed the lord's daughter. "For they're taking me off to the city in the morning, to wed my second cousin twice-removed. But I won't do it. If I can't marry the blacksmith's son, I won't marry anyone at all. I'll lie down and die first."

"So you want to marry the blacksmith's son," said the little man thoughtfully. "Does the blacksmith's son want to marry you?"

"He would if he knew me better," the girl said.

"I could help you," the little man said. "But you might have to put up with a bit of inconvenience. You might not like it."

"I'll put up with it," said the girl. "I wouldn't mind anything if it came out all right in the end."

So the little man gave her two small berries and told her to swallow them before she went to sleep that night. "You can leave the rest to me. You won't be going off to the city in the morning!" he said with a grin.

Early the next morning, the maid came up with the girl's breakfast tray. When she opened the door and went in, the tray dropped out of her hands. The girl's mother came running in, and when she saw what was in the room, she screamed and fainted right away. The lord heard all the racket and rushed in. There was his wife on the floor, and the maid, with the tray and dishes all at her feet, wringing her hands. He looked at the bed. His daughter wasn't there!

"Where could she have gone?" he shouted.

His wife raised her head from the floor. "Have you looked in the bed?" she said in a weak voice.

"I have!" said the lord grimly. "She's gone! The bed's empty."

"My love," said his wife, "it's not empty."

The lord went over to the bed and his lady came with him. The bed was not empty, though his daughter was not in it. In her place, with its head on the pillow and its forelegs on the silken coverlet, lay a little white dog.

"What's a dog doing in my daughter's bed?" shouted the lord. "Put it out in the hall at once!" And he started to do it himself. But his wife caught his arm.

"I don't think it's a dog," she said. "I very much fear it's our daughter."

"Have you gone mad?" the lord said angrily.

But his wife pointed out to him that the dog was wearing the blue silk nightgown that she had put on their daughter the night before. And hadn't the maid braided her hair with a blue satin ribbon? And wasn't the dog's little forelock all braided and tied exactly the same? It was plain to see that someone had put a spell on the girl and turned her into a dog. Just then the little dog chuckled with the daughter's own pleased chuckle and patted the lord on the cheek with its paw, just as his daughter always did with her hand.

"Oh, you little rascal," said the lord, never able to find it in his heart to be angry with his daughter for long. "Now what are we going to do?" One thing was clear and certain. They wouldn't be leaving the castle that day. So a messenger was sent to the second cousin twice-removed, to tell him not to expect them. The servants were told the girl was sick in bed with some sort of illness and nobody but the maid was to come in the room.

The lord called for his personal physician, though his wife and the maid told him it wouldn't do any good. The doctor looked at the dog and shook his head. "I don't see a young lady here," he said. "That's nothing but a dog."

The maid and his wife were right. The doctor was no use at all. An old woman came with herbs and powders, but all she could do was tell them the girl was bewitched. How to take the spell off, she didn't know.

The maids carried the news that the lord's daughter had taken sick to the village, and the blacksmith's son soon heard all about it. If he thought his heart was broken before, it was twice as bad when he thought the lord's daughter might die. He was hammering away at a bit of metal, not even noticing the iron had gone cold, when a shadow fell across the door. He looked up to see a little tiny man all dressed in green, with a red cap and red shoes.

"Have you seen the pretty daughter of the lord up at the castle?" the little man asked.

The blacksmith's heart jumped as if it were stuck with a pin, but all he said was "Yes."

"Has anyone told you that she's mortally ill?" the little man continued.

The blacksmith's son gave a great big sigh, but all he said was "Yes."

"Have you been up to the castle to ask about the lord's pretty daughter?" asked the little man.

The blacksmith's son shot him a glowering look. "No," he said.

"Do you know what's wrong with her?" asked the little man.

"I do not," said the blacksmith's son, throwing his hammer to one side. "Now, will you leave me in peace?"

The little man stayed right where he was. "Not yet," said he. "Why don't you go up to the castle and cure the lord's pretty daughter yourself?"

"Cure her!" shouted the blacksmith's son. "I'd lay down my life to cure her, the pretty young lady. How could someone like me do any good when they've had the lord's own doctor there to see her and he couldn't do a thing?"

"I know a way to cure her, if you'd like to try it," said the little man. "But answer me this question first. Would you like to marry the pretty young lady?"

"Are you crazy?" groaned the boy. "How could a blacksmith's son marry the daughter of a lord?"

"That's not what I asked you," said the little man. "I asked would you like to marry her?"

"I'd lie down and die before I'd marry anyone else!" cried the blacksmith's son.

Then the little man gave him two little berries, just like the ones he'd given the girl.

"Here's the cure for her sickness," he told the blacksmith's son. "Now, dress yourself up in your Sunday best, and make sure you don't try to cure the girl till the lord has given his promise you can marry her if you do."

The blacksmith's son cleaned himself up and dressed in his best clothes, then went straight to the castle and asked to see the lord.

"Well, who are you and what do you want?" the lord asked him with a frown.

"I'm the blacksmith's son."

When the lord heard who it was, he jumped straight from his chair and went for the boy, ready to throw him out with his own two hands. After all, it was the blacksmith's son at the bottom of all this trouble.

The blacksmith's son sidestepped the lord and said quickly, "I've come to cure your daughter."

Well, that made a difference. Now the lord was all smiles.

"But before I do it, I want permission to marry her," said the blacksmith's son.

"Never!" thundered the lord.

"Then I'll be on my way," said the blacksmith's son, and started for the door.

What could the poor lord do? He had to give in, and he knew it. So he did. "You can have her," said the lord to the blacksmith's son.

The little dog jumped from the bed and ran up to the blacksmith's son the minute he and the lord came into the room. The boy took the berries from his pocket and popped them into her mouth. Before you could say "Two and two is four," there stood the lord's daughter in the little dog's place!

She took the boy's hand in her own, and she turned to the lord and said, "I'm going to marry the blacksmith's son."

"Marry him, then!" grumbled the lord, not too unhappy about it since he had his daughter back again.

So the spoiled girl got her way in the end and married the blacksmith's son. The lord wasn't too ill-pleased, for he soon found his son-in-law was as likable a person as any he'd ever known. It all ended well, and that's all there is to tell of the lord's daughter and the blacksmith's son.

THE MARRIAGE OF TWO MASTERS

nce there was a girl named Aisatou Djili, who was so intelligent that she may have been the wisest person in the whole world. She was also extraordinarily beautiful, and all the young men wanted to marry her. But whenever they came to court her, it didn't go well. As soon as she started speaking, the suitor would become confused. She would have to tell him to go home. She was too intelligent, and nobody could understand her. She lived this way for a long time.

One day a man from the east heard about this woman. He thought he had to meet her for himself. He climbed onto his donkey and set out on the dusty road toward her village. It so happened that this very day Aisatou's father was traveling on the same road. He had been in the capital to do business, and now he was going home. He was riding on his horse, so it wasn't long before he overtook the young man.

"Peace be with you, Father," the young man called in greeting.

"And so with you," the father replied.

Aisatou's father asked the young man where he was going, and when it turned out they were going to the same place, they agreed they would travel together. "But who will carry whom?" the young man wondered aloud. "Will I carry you or will you carry me?"

Hearing these words, Aisatou's father began to think maybe this man was a little crazy. "Well, since you're riding a donkey and I'm riding a horse, surely we've no need to carry each other," he answered sternly.

"Of course you are right, Father," the young man replied politely.

After they had ridden for a while, the young man spoke again. "There's snow on the mountain," he observed.

Once again, Aisatou's father wondered if the man was completely sane. "How can there be snow on the mountain? It's the middle of the dry season and hot as an oven," he snapped.

"Yes, Father, that is true," responded the man.

Soon the travelers passed a small cotton field, surrounded by a sturdy fence. "Look at how beautifully this field is fenced!" the young man cried in admiration.

"Yes, it is a very sturdy fence," the father agreed. "It will last a full year."

A little later they passed a cotton field that stretched for acres and acres into the wilderness.

"That is a very big field," the young man observed, and the old man agreed with him.

"Father, concerning these two cotton fields — which would you prefer to own, the large one or the small one?"

"My son, do you take me for a fool? I would choose the large one, of course."

"Of course, Father."

As they continued down the road, they saw a funeral procession going in the opposite direction. After the mourners had passed out of hearing, the youth again asked a curious question. "Father, that man in the coffin, do you think he is living or dead?"

"I assure you, young man, he is dead."

"What a tragedy." The young man sighed, shaking his head.

At last they came to the village. Unfortunately the laws of hospitality demanded that Aisatou's father offer this odd stranger shelter for the night, and he reluctantly did so. The young man thanked him a thousand times but assured him he would be well lodged "in the home of the people," whatever that meant. Aisatou's father was relieved as he and the young man went their separate ways.

Aisatou was happy to see her father again, and after he had washed off the dust of the road and refreshed himself with a good dinner, she asked him to tell her all about his journey.

"I traveled with the strangest fellow today," her father began. "I think he must be a little out of his mind." He told his daughter about all the strange things the young man had said.

When Aisatou heard the story, she began to laugh. "Oh, Father, he isn't out of his mind — you just didn't understand him. When first he greeted you, he said, 'Who will carry whom? Will I carry you or will you carry me?' By this he meant that since you were traveling together, you should try to entertain each other with conversation. In this way you don't notice the hardships of the road much, and you are each carried along by the other.

"When he said that there was snow on the mountain, he meant that the hair on your head is white. You should have replied, 'Time has done this to me.'

"You passed two fields of cotton, one large and one small, and he asked you which you would prefer to own. You chose the larger one, but Papa, the larger one had no fence around it. Don't you see that anyone could steal from it or damage the crops? In the end the small field is sure to yield more cotton."

"What about when he asked if the man in the coffin was living or dead? Only a crazy person would ask such a question," her father insisted.

"What he was really asking was whether the man had left any children. When we have children, we can never die because our spirit lives on in them. Papa, I want to meet this man. Where is he staying?"

"He said he was staying 'in the home of the people,' wherever that is."

"By that he meant the mosque. He must be hungry, then, for there won't be any food in the mosque at this time of night. I am going to send him something to eat."

Aisatou packed a dozen boiled eggs and a bowl of porridge, which she gave to her father along with a gourd full of clean drinking water. "Take these to that young man, and ask him to come and visit me tomorrow," she said.

The father went to the mosque to find the young man. On his way he met an old beggar who asked him for something to eat and drink, so he gave him two eggs and filled his cup with water from the gourd.

At the mosque he found the young man, just as his daughter had predicted. He gave him the food and her message.

"Thank you a thousand times, Father. Tell your daughter that the year lacked two months and the river was at low tide, and that I will come to visit her tomorrow with my house in my hands."

Aisatou's father hurried home and delivered the message. "You see, my child, I told you this man is crazy. What was he talking about?"

"Father," she asked him, "whom did you meet on the way to the mosque?"

"I met an old beggar. Why do you ask?"

"Did you give him two eggs and fill his cup with water from the gourd?"

A puzzled expression passed over the old man's face. "Yes, I did. How in God's name did you know?"

"When the stranger said that the year lacked two months, he meant that two of the twelve eggs I sent him were missing. When he said the river was at low tide, this was to tell me that the drinking gourd was only half full. Tomorrow he is coming with his house in his hands. Father, he wants to marry me! When he asks your permission, you must say yes. This is the man I want to marry."

Soon after the wedding ceremony, Aisatou and her husband planted many fields of cotton, all with sturdy fences around them. They had many children and grew rich as kings. Have you ever met someone who was so intelligent you couldn't understand a word she said? This person is probably the great-great-great-great-great-grandchild of Aisatou Djili. May her spirit live forever.

Source Notes

The Serpent Slayer. Based on "The Serpent-Slayer" from *Sweet and Sour: Tales from China,* retold by Carol Kendall and Yao-wen Li (New York: The Seabury Press, 1978).

The Barber's Wife. Based on "The Barber's Clever Wife" from *Tales of the Punjab: Folklore of India,* by Flora Annie Steel (New York: Macmillan, 1894).

Nesoowa and the Chenoo. Based on the "The Chenoo Who Stayed to Dinner" from *More Glooscap Stories: Legends of the Wabanaki Indians,* by Kay Hill (New York: Dodd, Mead, 1970).

Clever Marcela. Based on "Clever Manka" from *The Shoemaker's Apron,* retold by Parker Fillmore (New York: Harcourt, Brace and Howe, 1920); "Cay Calabasa" from *Filipino Popular Tales,* by Dean S. Fanselar, in the Memoirs of the American Folk-lore Society series, Vol. 12 (Lancaster, Penn.: American Folk-lore Society, 1921); and "The Basil Plant" from *Folktales of Chile,* edited by Yolando Pino-Saavedra (Chicago: University of Chicago Press, 1967).

Sister Lace. Based on "Sister Lace" from *Favourite Folktales of China,* translated by John Minford (Beijing: New World Press, 1983).

The Rebel Princess. Based on "The King and the Emperor" from *Rabbi Nachman's Stories,* translated by Rabbi Aryeh Kaplan (Jerusalem: Breslov Research Institute, 1983); "The King and the Emperor" from *Nahman of Bratslav: The Tales,* translated by Arnold J. Band (New York: Paulist Press, 1978); and "The Faithful Lovers" from *The Hasidic Story Book,* by Harry Rabinowicz (London: Shem Tov Publications, 1984).

Beebyeebyee and the Water God. Based on "Beebyeebyee and the Water God" from *Tortoise the Trickster and Other Folktales from Cameroon,* by Loreto Todd (London: Routledge & Kegan Paul Ltd., 1979). Adapted by permission of Loreto Todd.

Kate Crackernuts. Based on "Kate Crackernuts" from *Folk-Lore,* Vol. I, 1890.

The Old Woman and the Devil. Based on "The Old Crone Who Was More Wiley than Iblees" from *Egyptian and Sudanese Folk-Tales,* retold by Helen Mitchnik (New York: Oxford University Press, 1978) and "The Old Woman and the Devil" from *Arab Folktales,* translated and edited by Inea Bushnaq (New York: Pantheon, 1986).

The Magic Lake. Based on "The Magic Lake" from *Latin American Tales: From the Pampas to the Pyramids of Mexico,* by Genevieve Barlow (New York: Rand McNally, 1966).

Grandmother's Skull. Based on "The Skull that Saved the Girl" from *The Eagle's Gift: Alaska Eskimo Tales,* by Knud Rasmussen (New York: Doubleday, Duran and Company, 1932).

Three Whiskers from a Lion's Chin. Based on "Crescent Moon Bear" from *Women Who Run with the Wolves,* by Clarissa Pinkola Estes (New York: Ballantine, 1992) and "A Discerning Old Faki" from *Egyptian and Sudanese Folk-Tales,* retold by Helen Mitchnik (New York: Oxford University Press, 1978).

Duffy the Lady. Based on "Duffy and the Devil" from *Popular Romances of the West of England,* collected and edited by Robert Hunt (London: Llanerch Enterprises, 1916).

Sun-Girl and Dragon-Prince. Based on "Sun-Maid and Dragon-Prince" from *Apples of Immortality: Folktales of Armenia,* by Leon Surmelian. Copyright © 1968 by the University of California Press. Adapted by permission of the University of California Press.

Staver and Vassilissa. Based on "Staver and Vassilissa" from *The Stolen Fire: Legends of Heroes and Rebels from Around the World,* by Hans Baumann, translated by Stella Humphries. Copyright © 1974 by Random House, Inc., and © 1988 by Elisabeth Baumann. Adapted by permission of Pantheon Books, a division of Random House, Inc., and by permission of Elisabeth Baumann.

Tokoyo. Based on "The Tale of the Oki Islands" from *Folk and Fairy Tales of Far-Off Lands,* by Eric and Nancy Protter (New York: Buell, Sloan and Pearce, 1965).

The Lord's Daughter and the Blacksmith's Son. Based on "The Laird's Lass and the Gobha's Son" from *Thistle and Thyme: Tales and Legends from Scotland,* by Sorche Nic Leodhas. Copyright © 1962 by LeClaire G. Alger and Holt, Rinehart and Winston. Adapted by permission of McIntosh & Otis, Inc., and by permission of Henry Holt and Company, Inc.

The Marriage of Two Masters. Based on "The Marriage of Two Masters" from *Folktales from the Gambia,* by Emil A. Magel (Washington, D.C.: Three Continents Press, 1984); "The Dream Interpreter" from *Jewish Stories One Generation Tells Another,* by Peninnah Scharma (Northvale, N.J.: Jason Aronson, Inc., 1987); and "The Farmer Who Found His Match in His Daughter-in-law" from *Egyptian and Sudanese Folk-Tales,* retold by Helen Mitchnik (New York: Oxford University Press, 1978).

ACKNOWLEDGMENTS

This book is not the first collection of folk and fairy tales about strong women. We discovered many of the stories in this book in these other wonderful anthologies of feminist folktales, and we thank their authors for bringing them to light:

Wise Women: Folk and Fairy Tales from Around the World, retold by Suzanne I. Barchers.

Clever Gretchen and Other Forgotten Folktales, retold by Alison Lurie.

The Skull in the Snow, retold by Toni McCarty.

Womenfolk and Fairy Tales, collected by Rosemary Minard.

The Maid of the North and *Tatterhood and Other Tales,* edited by Ethel Johnston Phelps.

We also wish to thank Barbara Rogasky, of Thetford, Vermont, for her excellent advice; Fred Hill, of the Fletcher Free Library in Burlington, Vermont, for his tireless interlibrary loan services; and Febe, Adele, Teresa, and Gladys for their help with "Three Whiskers from a Lion's Chin."